Broadmoor Castle

Mason Stone

Dedicated to those who believe that Love heals us.
And for my Pig, who knows.

Disclaimer
This is a work of fiction, and the persons, events and circumstances are fictitious. Certain passages refer to real places only to add color and verisimilitude to the story.

ISBN 978-1-989386-02-6

Cover image courtesy kellepics from Pixabay.

Chapter One The Seeker

The dreams were coming again --- the white lady standing --- her arms raised to heaven, her head thrown back, a glint, a flash of light from the choker on her throat.

Then the mist obscured the ancient stones below her.

Then there was the girl with golden hair looking straight into his eyes as if she knows his deepest desires--who knows they are lovers-- and he awakes, trembling.

He was almost used to them. He sometimes had trouble distinguishing between dream and reality. He ran his fingers through his hair and rubbed his eyes. It was morning.

This was Trevor Gower's first visit to the U.K. and he was excited to be a guest speaker at a conference to be held at Cambridge University.

His specialty was the esoteric traditions of Eastern and Western religion, and in Cambridge he was hoping to make some connections to enhance his knowledge of the ancient British sect called Druids.

Druidism held a special place in British folklore and history. Their mysterious rites held

in secret in forest groves continued to fascinate
note only scholars but the general public.

Trevor had a more personal interest in his
topic, however: his grandfather was said to have
been a Grand Druid High Priest of the Order of
Druids. He would have been one of the most
revered and high-ranking Druids in modern times.

And yet Trevor knew so little about him.
His own father was not a scholar and his mother
was not interested at all in esoteric lore. She was
the daughter of a Cornish miner and all she was
concerned with was putting food on the table and
paying the bills as they came due.

It had rained in the night and the slick
streets of the university town hissed with traffic
as he made his way to the presentation hall on
campus.

"Dr. Gower is it?" a friendly face inquired.
"Yes, yes it is," said Trevor to the older man
in a thick tweed jacket who extended a hand.
"Splendid! Won't you come this way? We
are so pleased you could come. We don't often see
Canadians here and have lost touch with the Royal
Ontario Museum since their elderly curator
passed. Do come in!"

Trevor was ushered into a sumptuous
room with oak paneling and plush maroon carpets
that served as a lounge for faculty.

"I am Reginald Applecrust and this is Clarinda Beehaven," the man said motioning to a prim lady seated on a horsehair sofa nearby.

"How do you do," said the lady with a nod, keeping her delicate hands on her lap.

"Is everything ready for the talk?" asked Trevor, unsure of what he should say or do.

"Yes. Our committee has the hall set up and the first registrants will be arriving shortly. Can I get you a cup of tea, Doctor—or do you prefer 'Professor' Gower?"

"That would be great Miss Beehaven—and I prefer 'Professor' as a title. 'Doctor' is a little pretentious for my taste.

Anyway, when people call me 'doctor' I get comments about which branch of medicine I practice, so then I have to explain that I am *not* that kind of doctor—and so on."

"Quite so," she remarked, pouring him hot tea in a dainty porcelain cup that was clearly antique, but with a tiny handle meant for much smaller fingers.

"Will you be staying on after the conference?" she continued politely.

"Actually, no. I have a busy semester in Toronto ahead of me and my students won't be happy if I start to leave gaps in the timetable."

"Certainly," said Miss Beehaven. "Do you have family? I'm sure they will miss you as well."

Her tone suggested she was being a little inquisitive with someone she had just met.
"No family at the moment," he said with as neutral a voice as he could muster.
What does she want? Why that question? he wondered. *Just nosy, perhaps?*

"Ah, here she is," announced Mr. Applecrust. "Janet will escort you to the hall now, Professor Gower. If there is anything more you need, just ask her."

Trevor bid goodbye to the two assistants and followed the girl striding swiftly down a long corridor lined with portraits of past alumni and faculty such as Isaac Newton, Charles Darwin, and Stephen Hawking—among many other famous men and women.

Founded in 1209, it is the second-oldest English-speaking university in the world, and is still regarded as Britain's top academic institution.

Trevor wanted more time to spend here, but suddenly the great hall opened and he found himself warmly welcomed as he took the stage.

"Thank you, I am delighted to be here at Cambridge today and hope that I have something to say that will be worthwhile. If you don't mind, I will use the projector to show some slides that will illustrate my key points a bit better for you."

The lights faded and the screen lit up with a legendary scene: the ring of giant megaliths at Stonehenge in Southwest England.

"We are all familiar with this magnificent standing stone circle and yet we remain ignorant of its builders and its true purpose.
Today I want to make some remarks that will possibly shed light on such ancient artifacts and do so in a holistic way that incorporates British culture and traditional belief."
And so he began. Trevor was a recognized authority on old British beliefs and religion from prehistoric times until the Renaissance arrived around 1650. He was comfortable with his topic and the audience seemed fascinated and attentive.

"In conclusion, I think there is every reason to believe that Druids are integral to our understanding of what Britons knew and believed about the mysteries of the Universe.
Thank you so much!"

The audience immediately got to its feet and thunderous applause filled the vast space of Cripps Hall.

The same young woman who had raced him down now took his arm and whispered in his ear.

"Would you be available for a question-and-answer period in the Great Study in—say, twenty minutes?"

Trevor answered in the affirmative.

To his relief, they served coffee, and freshly baked croissants and muffins.

Two young friends were chatting and glancing at him enough for him to notice. What he noticed most of all is that one of them was strikingly similar to the golden-haired damsel of his dreams the night before.

Strikingly.

They approached and greeted him.

"Professor Gower? I'm Jenna Watkins and this is my friend Brianna Hardy. We loved your talk, didn't we Brianna?"

The blonde nodded and looked straight at Trevor.

"We have some questions—well, *I* do, since I have a paper on pagan religion to finish in three weeks," said Jenna.

"First of all, are you saying that Stonehenge and similar sites can be correlated with Druid rituals at some distant date in the past?" She was standing close and looking up into his face.

Luckily, Trevor was used to dealing with students who could be quite pushy and insistent when they wanted something.
Not like the well-mannered kids he knew in school and university.

"Yes, Jenna, I *am*. And I'll tell you why."

Trevor went on to cite his sources and references that he found contributed to his current opinion.

All the while, Brianna sipped her tea, watching him intently as he moved his hands and shifted his weight.
Suddenly Trevor seemed aware of her and unconsciously moved to include her in the little circle of conversation.
"So what are you studying, Brianna?"
"Medicine. At Birmingham. My last year actually. Then need to find an internship somewhere.
I live up in the Midlands—which is both good and bad. Good--in that it is not so rushed and hectic as bigger cities, bad in that good placements are hard to find. And don't pay as well."
"I'm trying to convince her to move to London," said Jenna breezily. "Then I have an excuse to

move to London, since I can't possibly afford it on my own."

Jenna was looping Brianna's arm with hers and it was clear they were warm friends.

"When do you return to…?" Trevor wanted to say 'Midlands' but Brianna saved him.

"Shrewsbury; well, outside a few miles in a little village called Briar Hill. We run a small B&B called Wildswallows—my sister, brother-in-law, and me.

I take the bus to town and then the train to Birmingham where I stay over in a university dorm three nights a week."

Brianna felt suddenly self-conscious, as if she were telling her whole life story to this tall Canadian for some reason.

"When will you come back to the U.K., Professor?" said Jenna.

"That's an interesting question," said Trevor. "I hadn't really thought about it."

"Well, you should give it some thought," Jenna said. "I have a feeling that this is where you belong."

Trevor didn't look at Jenna first when she said that—he looked instead at Brianna.

His whole body shivered in a very subtle way, as if an electrical current flowed from her body to his body—and back again, repeatedly.

"I would like to come back to do research here. Would you consider giving me your e-mails so I at least know *some*body when I do."

Trevor seemed taller, and his strong frame and blue eyes made an impression in Brianna's memory.

She would later tell Jenna that she believed in Fate, that everything happens for a reason.

But right now, he was leaving for Canada and she was leaving for Shropshire.

"Goodbye for now, Professor," said Jenna taking his hand and giving it a playful shake.

"Please call me Trevor."

Brianna held out her hand—perhaps to mimic Jenna—but in any case Trevor suddenly, unexpectedly bowed to her, and softly kissed the back of her hand.

Jenna giggled and Brianna blushed.

He threw his raincoat over his head as he stepped into the typical English rain, and quickly entered a taxi taking him directly to Heathrow--a distance of 72 miles, taking about 90 minutes if traffic was good.

He thought about Brianna most of the way.

***

Trevor could not forget his dream girl—now she had a name! Brianna! But what did it all mean?

On his desk lay the artifacts that had been discovered in a hidden compartment in the wall of the library when Trevor's father was alive. They were shipped to him with no explanation of what to do with them. But he knew he was meant to have them.

That is when his direction in life seemed to change forever. As if everything had led him to that moment.

He now held the strange object in his hand. It was cast metal--perhaps bronze--with a patina of mossy green--ending in a talon or claw that clasped a small crystal ball.

It was a *dorje* or *vajra*--an ancient tool used by sadhus and shamans of the Far East he had learned. *Vajra* means 'thunderbolt', hinting at its immense power in the hands of an initiate.

But how would such an object be obtained by his grandfather J. Rossili Gower? And *why?*

Suddenly Trevor Gower wondered who he was and who his ancestors were. Living in Toronto-- formerly the town of York, Ontario founded in 1791 by British colonists--there was a shroud of mystery hanging over his own past.

At nearly forty years of age he began to contemplate the fact that he was still unmarried, childless, successful in his teaching career--but unsatisfied with his life.

His work as a Philosophy and History professor at the private all-girls Earlsdale College had led to a fascination with esoteric religion and occult knowledge.

In particular, it was the history of his British ancestors and that ancient land of stone circles and megaliths, Celtic mysteries and Druid priests, and fabulous legends like King Arthur and the Knights of the Round Table.

Some of it was folklore but much of it had historical evidence to support the stories. Trevor had dreamed of visiting the Britain from whence his ancestors came. But he had no idea where to begin—even if he took time off to explore those fabled isles.

Is anyone still alive who might remember his grandfather? Perhaps there was some stranger who might shed light on his family's past.

***

Professor Gower was startled out of his reverie by a sharp knock at his office door. It was that annoying student again.

"Professor, could you please explain why I only got 65% on my term paper. I put weeks of effort into it and I deserve better than a 'C' grade!"

"Come in, come in," said Trevor. "You know I would like to give you a better mark but your work is about average for this level of difficulty. Your references are not convincing—did you read all of the sources you cited in your bibliography?"

The student was not paying attention; her gaze was focused on the *dorje* on the corner of his desk on top of a flurry of papers.

"What is *that*?" Sanjita said with a nervous laugh.

"That is an artifact that belongs to my family," said Prof. Gower.

"I saw them in India before I came to Canada. In the temple. The priest used them in certain rituals. We were told it has magical powers," she said.

"That's what I would like to find out myself," Trevor said. "Perhaps I will take a trip somewhere and see what I can dig up."

"Be careful, Professor! There are things in this world that are kept in shadow for a reason!"

"You may be right, Sanjita. Now let's take a look at this paper and I will make suggestions for improving your skill for the next time."

After she had gone and the sun had set behind the trees, Trevor remained at his desk fingering the strange metal object clasping its transparent crystal.

Why had Grandfather hidden this where it was likely to never be found? He was a curio and antique collector all his life...what did he find out? Why was his death so sudden and mysterious?

Trevor had far more questions than answers.

The last glint of gold light came through the window and fell on the crystal. Lifting it closer he noticed there were tiny gold filaments embedded inside the ball that he had not noticed before. But in the sunset they sparkled intensely and gave him a strange feeling that he had lately—that Destiny or Fate was catching up with him—and he'd better be ready!

***

"John, I think I need some time off to do some research," Trevor said.

John Green was the headmaster at Earlsdale-- and had been so for many years. He knew Trevor well, and had been waiting for this to come.

"What do you have in mind, Trevor? England? You've always been enthralled by England and its ancient folklore and culture."

"Exactly. There is only so much that can be done from a desk or library table. I need to get to those marvelous archives at Cambridge and see

what they say about the Druids and Nature
worship—'paganism' is what many call it."

"How much time do you need?" John asked.
"Well, John, if I take a year off on sabbatical that
will let you find someone to take my classes
through the entire year without interruption.
That supply teacher—that young lady—
ah…Heather. She would work out well I think."

"It *would* be good to let some of the new
teachers get a crack at handling a long
assignment," John replied. "And I like her. The
girls like her too."

"Then it's agreed?" asked Trevor.

"We're going to miss you. Come back with
stories to tell us about your adventures!"

The two men shook hands warmly and Trevor
stepped into the warm night a free man--who was
going to get paid to do his dream job of
uncovering the mysteries of the past!
He packed aimlessly, his head in a cloud after he
had made the booking with Air Canada to fly to
Heathrow once more.

His dark blue passport lay on the table beside
his wallet. He left the apartment key with Mrs.
Inglis--the caretaker's wife.
Ready or not—England here I come!

Chapter Two   England

Trevor had not planned this; it was a spur of the moment thing really. Maybe that had to do with Brianna and Jenna, but it was his wish to take time to go to England to do primary research for years now. Only now he had another source of motivation.

He knew that the object and the parchment that accompanied it had an esoteric purpose. He also knew that his grandfather had entrusted it to his father—who had hidden it in the library and never bothered to mention it again except to say it was secret knowledge..

And it was--until Trevor found the latch that opened the locked box. But not even a learned scholar in mystical arts could readily identify what these artifacts were intended for.
Secrets are intended to stay secret. Only this was his family he was dealing with.
Although Trevor was passingly acquainted with ancient languages and symbols, such codes and ciphers on this document were that much harder to crack.
Assuming this was a code, it was made to hide a message or a revelation or a purpose that may be of real importance to historians.

He made a copy of all the strange glyphs and writing from the original—then placed it back in its compartment and shut it firmly. There would be no one who knows of it--he decided--as he packed himself for his journey.

"I'm in London," Trevor said into the phone.
"I'm taking the train to Cambridge and will do a couple of days of intense research in the libraries there. Are you able to come down?"

Brianna replied in the negative. Too busy.

Trevor was disappointed but tried to not let his voice show it.

"Very well. I will let you know when I'm done here and then take the train to Shrewsbury. I look forward to our meeting again, Brianna."

She must have said something, as his head lifted, and he said: "Thank you. I hope so too," then hung up.

He had to find someone who was expert in old Celtic dialects and script. The parchment was at least early Middle Ages—that would make it over a thousand years old!
Perhaps old Applecrust might know whom to see.

***

The English rain is often a mist that slightly obscures the vision; so it was only when Jenna came right up to him that Trevor recognized her.

"Professor Gower? Remember me?" Jenna was smiling and her even white teeth formed a dazzling smile that had a hidden meaning that Trevor did not immediately discern.
Not until she took his arm in hers and marched them to the shelter of the student center coffee place.

Trevor had kept himself rather isolated over recent years—he was not even dating.
So when an attractive young woman was giving him her full attention, he was awkward and a bit tongue-tied.

"I knew you would come back to us," Jenna said confidently. "And here you are!"

"I was on my way to the library do some research. How's that paper going? Have you finished it?"

"I would *love* for you to review it before I submit it. I'm so bad with writing and footnoting."

"Oh sure. Let's have a look."

Jenna opened her satchel but was looking at Trevor with mischief in her eyes.

"What's it like working at an all-girls school?
Don't you get a lot of attention--as a handsome
male teacher that they can look up to?"

Trevor wasn't expecting this question.

"Don't you ever get tempted to...explore a
more...um...meaningful relationship with a
student?"
Trevor mumbled something about professional
ethics, but Jenna was on a roll.

"Why don't we play a little game? I'll be one of
your favorites. You be...who you are.
And you are helping me with my term paper,
but inside you are starting to heat up as you feel
my breath on your cheek and my lips are...".

"Whoa, Jenna. Wait! I'm not thinking anything
but how to fix this assignment of yours."

But Jenna knew his eyes were telling a different
story. His five o'clock shadow could not hide the
rush of blood that had come to his face.

"Have you talked to Brianna?" she said,
changing the topic.

"She said she's tied up with school and can't see
me right now."

"So you called her before you called me?" she teased.

"I don't have your mobile. You didn't give it to me."

"Well—I will now!"

"First of all," Trevor said, "Your formatting is dreadful. The single most important feature of a piece of writing is paragraphing."

"I love it when you talk dirty to me!" Jenna said.

"We have to do this, Jenna. So please listen to what I am saying. And where is your thesis continuity here? You make claims that are unsupported or don't relate to your thesis."

"I told you I am not good at this. And you are *so* good at it. Help me revise or even rewrite the whole thing, won't you Trevor?"

"Ok, look, Jenna. I will go over it tonight with a red pencil and flag areas that need work. I will write some comments here and there, and then I will meet you for lunch tomorrow and go over what you have to do. How's that sound?"

Jenna was pouting and biting her bottom lip in a way that seemed to make Trevor restless.
"If that is what you think is best, Professor, then I guess I'll have to follow your lead."

"What time do Admin offices close around here?" he said. "I've got to talk to them about my research before they all go home."

"Well, it's tea-time. They will close around six."

"Can you point me to the Main Administrative Building? I really should get going, Jenna."

She drew close to him as she turned and pointed.

"I'll text you, Trevor. You will need to get a SIM card for your phone to work. I'll help you with that tomorrow when we meet."

Again—that smile of hers! She knew he was weakening.

"Until tomorrow. Bye Jenna."

Then he was gone as the dim afternoon slipped into a grey sunset.

A small smile stole across her face, and she turned toward the dormitory where she shared a room with Samantha—another English Lit major.

"Oh my gawd, you are such a *flirt*, Jenna Jones." Samantha was a chirpy blonde bundle of energy and conversation who was a perfect complement to Jenna's dark hair and cat eyes.

"Well, why not? Before he disappears into the countryside to visit Brianna, why can't I have a bit of fun with him?"

"Did you...?"

"...get a selfie with him? Of course!"

"Ohh, he's handsome. He has nice eyes and his hair lays on his forehead in such an appealing way! Were you thinking what you are usually thinking?"

"Sex? Definitely! I will give you fair notice when I need the room for myself and my guest."

"How come I never have these kind of opportunities?" Samantha groaned.

"Because you are a *nice girl*—and I'm not!" said Jenna triumphantly. She went on.

"I'm meeting him for lunch and he will have corrected my piece of shit assignment for me—as a favor."

"If he has a brother, you'll tell me, right?"

The two laughed and brushed their hair before going down to the dining hall for supper.

The next morning Jenna received a text message that Trevor was leaving immediately for Shrewsbury from Euston Station in London.

I am sorry we cannot meet as agreed; Brianna says I must come at once.
I have left your paper—with corrections—at the Student Centre at Pembroke College at the desk. Please ask for it there.
E-mail me if you have questions:
tgower@earlsdalecollege.ca

***

The train trip would be about two to three hours with occasional stops on its 139 mile journey to the lovely English countryside now showing autumn colors of red, orange and gold.

Trevor barely had time to pack and get to Euston Station as it was near Regent's Park and the British Museum. The traffic in London is abominable for visitors but familiar to cabbies.

He caught the 8:34 and found a seat near the window.

Slurping a double-shot cappuccino Trevor pondered what had frightened Brianna. She had said there was a message left in the mailbox at Wildswallows with weird symbols and an ominous text: *Stay far from Broadmoor if you value your life.*

Broadmoor Castle. Trevor knew nothing about it. Was in private hands for hundreds of years.

Current owners: unknown. Current use and purpose: unknown.

A bigger mystery was why Brianna would have anything to do with it.

Obviously someone wanted her to stay away for reasons that Brianna would be expected to know.

Trevor hardly knew her and certainly did not know her background story, but he was eager to find out.

He knew she was a medical student in Birmingham—a major English city fifty miles east of Shrewsbury yet still considered West Midlands. The University had a famous clock tower.

More than that was still a blank to be filled in.

The sweep of River Severn came into view as the train pulled into Shrewsbury Station and hissed to a stop.

Trevor half-expected to see her—waving or something, but the platform was empty as he stepped into the street.

Take Blakie's Taxi waiting just outside and tell the driver you are going to Briar Hill and offer him ten quid max. See you when you get here.

The text message was clear enough.

The drive south was full of farms and pasture, cows black and white against the green--with the distant hills appearing now out of the morning mist. Trevor rolled the window down to smell the fresh country air and listen to the meadowlarks sing.

He directed the driver to Wildswallows Inn-- which was not hard to find in an English village with one main road.

He fished a ten-pound note out of his wallet and yanked his suitcase out of the trunk ('boot' in England, the driver reminded him).

He had arrived and feeling of coming home swept over him. England was the land of his own people and it was in his blood.

Chapter Three   Wildswallows

Trevor knocked and entered the portico that served as a lobby for the inn.

The owners were Beryl and Bill—Beryl was her older sister by some six-and-a-half years. She greeted Trevor.

"Welcome," she said with a lilting voice common in the Midlands.

"You enjoyed the trip up, did you?"

"Yes, thank you. I was rather rushed this morning."

"I bet you could do with a bit of lunch," she said, and at the mention of food, Trevor stood up straighter and smiled.

"Brianna is gone to the bakery to fetch some things and will be back directly. Let me show you your room."

From his bedroom he had a sweeping view of the countryside that fell away from the low sandstone ridge upon which the village was situated.

The room was simply furnished and the bed looked comfortable and the sheets and towels smelled of fresh air. He slipped out of his overcoat and changed his shoes for sandals.

There was a sink and bath down the hall, as well as--the 'loo' she had called it. His British

Rough Guide said toilets were called 'WC' or 'water closet' and were enclosed in a tiny closet beside the main washroom. He would share these facilities with other guests who might also be staying on the second floor.

He heard quick footsteps as someone mounted the stairs.

"Trevor! I'm so glad you came, so glad you're here!" She drew close and hugged him briefly.

"You must be knackered. Let's have some lunch and give you a good cup of English tea. It's done wonders for our nation for over two hundred years!"

Brianna led him by the hand downstairs into a charming dining room with lace curtains and an ample dining table that would seat eight.

"You've not been in England long I take it?"

Now Bill had entered and seated himself at the head of the table, extending his hand to Trevor.

"Fresh off the boat," Trevor quipped.

"Good. Let's get you off on the right foot. We country folk eat simple. Egg and sausage, toast and homefries. You Canadians prefer bacon, I believe. We have some right tasty bacon as well."

"We can make you a coffee, love, if you prefer that," added Beryl.

"He's having *tea*, Sis," interjected Brianna. "He's going to become an Englishman while he's here," she continued, as if she were taking charge of everything Trevor from the get-go.

"Take him to The Root & Branch, Brianna. He'll be wanting a pint of real English beer," said Bill.

"That would be great," said Trevor. "But later. It's still before noon."

"How about a walk in the village to get yourself oriented?" said Brianna.

"Do I need an umbrella?" Trevor said.

"Nah," Bill said. "It don't rain every day in England. Just Mond'ys, Tuesd'ys, Wednesd'ys, Thursd'ys and most Frid'ys," he said with a grin.

The air was freshly washed by a brief morning shower that had passed, and the warm sun of September was drying up the puddles already.

"Show me the note, Brianna."

Brianna unfolded the rough paper she took from her purse.

"This is peculiar—it has a Celtic protection symbol which has a double meaning."

Trevor was studying the strange message.

"This is an axe or double-bladed weapon. It means protection, but it also means something deeper—symbolic death and transformation."

"Am I to die, then?" said Brianna looking fearful.

"I certainly hope not…no. Of course not! And it can be taken different ways.

For that matter, so can these words. 'If you value your life' may not be a threat at all.

It might be a warning to protect yourself from whatever is happening at Broadmoor by avoiding the place.

I think we need to investigate a bit more about what that might be."

"Marnin' Miss Hardy," said the old baker, setting out his sign on the sidewalk that advertises his tasty wares. "Come in and try this bun— they're fresh hot from the oven!"

Brianna and Trevor were so impressed that they bought a half dozen to take back to the inn.

"I want to rent a car in town, so we can come and go. I have a feeling we're going to be doing a lot of travelling around these hills," Trevor said.

"You won't leave me alone, will you?"

Brianna stepped close to him and looked up into his face, her blue eyes catching the light.

He gently touched her face and brushed a wisp of hair from her forehead.

"Look. I'll tell you the truth, Brianna. The real reason I have come to England is to find out more about my family history. There are some puzzling matters that need to be resolved.

Of course, there is endless opportunity to do further research in pagan and Celtic culture."

He was careful not to mention the encounter with Jenna at Cambridge. It wasn't relevant, he'd decided.

"Perhaps my story and your story are entwined in some unforeseeable way," he went on.

Anyway, I am here because you invited me and I will not leave you to face the unknown alone."

Brianna threw her arms around his waist and Trevor pulled her tight to him, kissing her lightly on the top of her head.

"My Dad did that to me when I was a child," she said.

"Where are your parents now?" Trevor asked.

"That's what I want to find the answer to, Trevor. What happened to them. If my sister knows, she has never told me anything. I feel like an orphan. Do you know how that feels?"

"Why don't you tell me your story, Brianna?"

***

"Where should I begin?" she said.
They had found a rather cozy and warm corner in
the pub where they could have a bit of privacy.

Trevor was watching her face over the rim of the
pint of ale he was enjoying.

"I was born here, in the village, twenty-eight
years ago. My parents were well-off and we lived
at Broadmoor Castle which my mother had
inherited from her father—Lord Trethewey of
Strathmore, a tenth generation nobleman going
back to the Norman Invasion.
	Broadmoor is actually a Norman castle—built
to consolidate King William's dominance over
Anglo-Saxon England."

	The food came, and Trevor ordered another
pint.

	"I have an older sister—as you know—so
growing up in the castle was not so lonely. There
were so many rooms to play hide and seek in.
	We had stables and horses so I grew up loving
anything equestrian. I think I miss the horses
more than anything."

	"What happened?"

	Brianna was thinking that Trevor had a way of
focusing with intensity--that both put you on the

spot, and flattered you with the attention at the same time.

"Sometime during the winter after my sixth birthday, my world of being the princess of the castle came to a dramatic and sudden end.

They let my uncle—The Earl of Trent—to take charge of us, vulnerable young girls suddenly left alone. The Earl and Countess of Trent live in the valley on their own estate.

We wanted to stay in the castle. We also wanted some explanation of what happened to Mum and Dad."

Brianna's voice caught. She reached across and lifted Trevor's pint and gulped half of it down.

Then she went on.

"We were placed in the local priory school close to Shrewsbury, and so far as we knew the castle was closed up.

The earl told us that my parents had been killed in a terrible accident and that we would be staying with them—at least until we turned eighteen.

I suppose we should be grateful but I have always had a feeling—more like a strong intuition—that the *whole* story was being kept from us.

It might be that the Earl and Countess did not know themselves.

It might be that there were layers of secrecy that are not meant to be revealed.

I am convinced that whatever is going on at Broadmoor is shady and possibly criminal, Trevor. You hear stories, understand?"

"And no one advised you of your legal position as heiress to the castle?"

"I haven't had the time or energy to look into it," she said. "I've put all my power into finishing my medical training.

I moved into residence at Birmingham to get away from the memory of this place. It is so dark when I think of it."

"And what about Wildswallows? Does that belong to your family as well?"

"It was purchased by my sister and her husband using trust money that was given from my family estate after my parents were declared... legally...*dead*."

"Don't think I am prying into your business—or scheming in any way to get your money—but, what happened to *your* share of the trust fund?"

"Uncle Jeffrey would know. If I need money, I go to him. That's how I paid my tuition for seven years of university."

"So you have no idea of how much of the family fortune remains, and more importantly—what the fate of Broadmoor Castle is going to be?" Trevor asked.

Brianna shifted uncomfortably.

"I've burdened you with my family business, Trevor. I'm sorry."

"Not at all. But I think somebody should start to ask some questions."

"I'm afraid, Trevor. Look at that note! It relates explicitly to Broadmoor...and to *me*!!"

"Then we shall be very quiet about all of this," he said.

Trevor took her hand in a warm reassuring way.

"I have a plan, actually, that might give us a reason to visit the castle--and take a look for ourselves."

***

"I'm still not sure I can get used to this," Trevor said. "Steering wheel on the wrong side and driving on the left instead of the right.

And these roundabouts are killers! We don't have them in Canada. We just have large intersections with traffic lights and it all works perfectly!"

"You'll be just fine, Trev," Brianna said cheerily. "Anyone with your intellect can figure out how to drive on English roads, I have no doubt!"

He needed her confidence to get him through town and out on the A49 heading south through Bayston Hill then onto the hills beyond. The Welsh border was only ten miles to the west.

Once the traffic thinned out, Trevor was more
at ease.

"So what's this plan of yours, professor?"

Trevor smiled at the reminder. He was on
vacation—in effect—for a whole year, with pay.
He wanted to make it count for something.

"I am a scholar of Celtic culture in Britain, but
that does not preclude me from other historical
research.

Since I am new to the area, it can be assumed
that I am doing a local study into customs,
traditions, architecture and lifestyle..."

"You mean 'castles' as well," said Brianna.

"Exactly. Castles and manors, ancestry and
records of families both noble and common.

In order to be accurate, I will need to visit and
take notes and photographs. The usual things."

The highway started to rise noticeably as they
entered the dark forest of the Shropshire Hills.

"There!" said Brianna suddenly pointing.

Trevor turned the four-wheel drive hard onto a
gravel drive that ran between the dark spruce on
either side.

The road opened into a wide circle that would
bring visitors to the great arching doorway of this
ancient building but they were forced to stop by a

high, wrought-iron gate and fence that was
securely padlocked.

There were no vehicles inside the enclosure
and there were no tire tracks in the muddy area
where they put the car in 'P' and turned off the
motor.

"Now what?" Brianna whispered, as if someone
were listening, someone could hear their arrival.

Neither of them noticed the CCTV cameras
mounted on both the gatepost and on a tree just
outside the area they stood in.

"Well we're not going in, that's obvious. And
we're not going to trespass—at least, not *this*
time," said Trevor.

"I want to get some shots of the house from this
angle, and just make some preliminary observations of the front and the grounds."

A white tin sign was wired to the fence and
simply said '*Private*'.

The sun was setting fast and the shadows grew
long so Trevor adjusted the camera settings to
capture the dwindling light.

As darkness fell, an opalescent full moon rose
behind the turrets, giving the castle a
mysterious—or perhaps creepy atmosphere.

They took a few steps to the left, which allowed them to see through another corbelled archway to the center courtyard.

Suddenly Brianna gasped. Her finger pointed to the opening and Trevor followed with his eyes.

On the farther turret wall—beyond the gravel courtyard—was a woman, dressed in shimmering white, unearthly in her slow graceful step.

"Do you see that?" she whispered.

"Getting it on video," he replied.

"Who *is* she?" Brianna was trembling uncontrollably.

"You never told me Broadmoor had a ghost," said Trevor, trying not to show his nervousness.

"There's a legend, or local tale...whatever you want to call it. My Mum mentioned it once when we girls were in a fright over something we had experienced in one part of the castle."

"Well, whoever she is...she's vanished into the moonlight. Perhaps we should be getting home."

"Please, Trevor! Broadmoor Castle was once my home. Help me to get it back!"

Chapter Four   The Order

"The food here at Wildswallows is so good—I think I will stay for good!" quipped Trevor at breakfast.

"Fine by us," said Bill. "Hate to say it, but we like our own cooking, too!"

Brianna had left early to catch the morning train in town. The bus stopped in several villages on the way to Shrewsbury but made a quick trip into the train station, since it carried commuters travelling to various towns in the Midlands on its way to Birmingham.

Trevor saw his opportunity to ask questions, but he was very conscious of not opening a can of worms.

"I am considered an expert in old English beliefs such as Wicca and Druidism," he started.

"This is a superb chance for me to find out more about this part of England.

Of course, I know about the English Civil War and that this town was solidly Royalist."

"Oh so you know about the traitor who opened the gate at St. Mary's Lane to let the Roundhead bastards take the town!"

Bill's face turned red and his fist clenched with emotion.

"That was circa 1645, I think," Trevor said evenly.

"We never forget up here in the counties," Bill said. "We have a history and we're proud of it.
D'you know the Industrial Revolution started near here? The first iron bridge in Britain was built over the Severn, but a mile from the old Market Hall."

"I hear Charles Darwin was born and went to school here," said Trevor.

"The school was built by Edward VI in 1658 although it is now a library; Darwin's bronze effigy sits at the entrance on a pedestal. Clive of India went to the same school."

Trevor was getting a bit closer to his goal.

"I suppose you've got ghosts and apparitions in some of these places?" he said.

"Oh, ghosts aplenty," said Bill. "Take The Prince Rupert Hotel on High Street. Crawling with spirits. St. Mary's Church..."

"Broadmoor Castle?" said Trevor innocently. "It's not too far from Briar Hill I believe."

Beryl spoke for the first time in the conversation.

"Aye. There's a ghost there. Likely more than one I shouldn't doubt."

Trevor turned to face her, looking for a hint of something that would support Brianna's incredible assertion that it had been their home as girls.

"We don't go up there," said Bill in a low voice.

"Can you tell me anything about its history?" Trevor said, trying to conceal his excitement.

"It belonged to a certain family…" Bill started.

"Our family," said Beryl with a loud voice. "Until someone took it from us, just throwing my sister and me into the street!
We still have no idea what happened up there. All we know is our parents disappeared off the face of the earth and our home was no more!"

Tears came suddenly and Bill moved closer to his wife to comfort her.
"There, there, pet…it's all in the past. We've got a good life here."
But Beryl had opened the door to a flood of grief and anger that would not be easily closed.

"Somebody *knows*! Somebody has the key to why my father—Lord Trethewey of Strathmore— disappeared so suddenly. He would never abandon his family—I just know something wicked has taken place. And a wall of silence and conspiracy has fallen on this village."

Trevor had wanted to show them the artifacts from his library, the strange codes and objects, but this was now out of the question.

He had brought them--but kept them safely stowed in a locked case buried in his luggage. He wasn't sure himself about why they needed to be brought to England. He just knew they had to be here.

Beryl apologized and hastily cleaned up the dishes and began washing in the kitchen.

Bill looked embarrassed.
"Their uncle, the Earl, took 'em in. Gave 'em a respectable home and made life a little bit bearable.
But we got naught to go on so far as explaining what did happen, and why."
Bill's voice trailed away and Trevor decided to leave it for now.

"What time is Brianna due back? I'll run into town and meet her at the train," said Trevor.

"Oh, she is usually back by six o'clock if she gets her train in Birmingham. She sends us a text if she's going to be late.

You can save her another 45 minutes travel time if you can pick her up. We'd all appreciate that, Trevor," said Bill.

"No problem. That's why I've got the car. See you later. I think I'll stop into The King's Arms in Shrewsbury for a pint of their legendary ale. See what I can find out about...local history."

Trevor swung onto the highway and gunned it for town.

***

A shadowy figure was standing in the inner courtyard of Broadmoor Castle. Something silver flashed in its hand. A man's voice rose and fell in what seemed like chanting.

Abruptly he turned and entered the castle through an archway and a heavy door could be heard to slam shut.

Deep in the stony fortress were rooms and halls that had once served other purposes.

Now it was the home of The Order of Wolfbane and its dark-haired chieftain Rodann.

Their mission as he defined it was to restore the throne of Britain to its rightful lineage—not through Alfred the Great of Wessex, but through Arthur of Camelot, the last of the Celtic warrior-kings and high-priest of the mystical Druids of England.

Fourteen hundred years of British history had given the throne to the wrong people: Germans from Saxony and Hanover, Dutch and French interlopers who--through marriage or invasion--brought their culture to Celtic Britain and all but obliterated the true cultural roots and traditions.

The Order of Wolfbane would correct that; Wolfbane would set the record straight and affirm what *was*--even before the Roman occupation, and which even Caesar could not destroy.

The New would arise here—in this castle in northwest England--with members from nearby Wales, Cheshire, Wiltshire, The Midlands, and even Scotland and Ireland.

Thirteen swords were pointed at the *sangraal*, the Grail cup in the very center of the round table that flashed in the light of blazing fires set in four enormous fireplaces in the Great Hall.

Rodann intoned The Affirmation and twelve other voices followed.

I affirm and swear by the powers of Heaven and Earth my allegiance to Arthur, true King of Britain, and offer now my body and soul to the return of The Holy Grail to its rightful place at his right hand.

Thirteen swords were lifted in the orange light and smoke, then placed back on the polished wood and copper surface of a table that resembled nothing so much as a great battleshield with thirteen places for thirteen brave knights dressed in splendid mail and helmets, each with its own colored vestments of crimson or yellow or cobalt or purple.

This was their council table. This was their center. This was where The New Order would be birthed.

***

"Tell me about Trent—the earl who took you in after you were dispossessed of Broadmoor."

"Jeffrey and Jodie were good to us, they treated us like their own daughters," Brianna began.

"The Earl and Countess of Trent inherited lands and wealth from a great grandfather who had rendered service to the Crown and been granted two hundred acres of fields and woods known in these parts as the Abbey Grange."

"Why do you call him 'Uncle Jeffrey'?" said Trevor.

"Why, he is a Hardy, he is my father's younger brother," she said.

"He is wealthy in his own right," Brianna went on. "He is very good with investments and has made a fortune from mines in Indonesia and Brazil. Pity they have no children of their own."

"So to whom will the money go—once they are gone?"

"I have no idea. I really don't. I suppose they have a charity or something in mind. Perhaps the church."

Trevor drained his beer and called for another. The Root & Branch was often full as it was one of the few hangouts for both young and old in Briar Hill.

As the autumn advanced and night grew colder, the warmth and congeniality of a traditional English pub could not be matched.

"Is there anyone I've missed in your family tree?" Trevor said.

Brianna shifted uneasily and held the stem of her wineglass, lifting and swirling its contents.

"There is my brother. He was older than either of us girls. He often fought with our parents and spent his time storming around the castle."

"Where is he now?" said Trevor.

"I don't know. He was ordered out of the home years ago after a particularly nasty confrontation with my Mother. I was too young at the time to understand what was being said, but I knew from the tone of their voices and the words they used—harsh words—that he would not be coming back."

"Your Mum never spoke about it to you?"
"Never. And I was too polite or too shy to ask."

"I suppose I should tell you about my family,
since I have been nosing into yours," Trevor said.

"I am an only child, born and raised in Toronto
Canada. I attended public school and then the
University of Toronto, my alma mater. I majored
in British History with a minor in Religious Study
of Traditional Religion in Britain.
What I mean is Wicca, Druidism, paganism—all
those things the Church hated and suppressed.
I wanted to find out what the original Britons
believed and how they lived.
Some of that is because my ancestors are
British and some of it just because I am morbidly
curious about Earth religions and magic and
such."
Brianna was smiling.

"I like that," she said. "Someone should be
looking into it. We've become so modern, so
worldly in Britain. I think many of us wonder
about our cultural roots. But we're too damn busy
trying to make a living to give it a thought.
Cheers!"

Brianna lifted her glass and clinked his.

"Where's your Mum and Dad?" she continued.

"Both dead, unfortunately. Killed in the Rwandan Civil War in 1994. They were missionaries in Africa and were teachers at a school when sudden hostilities broke out between the dominant Hutus and the minority Tutsis.

Rebels invaded the village where they had been placed and slaughtered everyone—every child, adult, and...my parents.

I did not hear from them and when I wrote to the bishop in Nairobi I got a short one-sentence e-mail that I will never forget."

"Oh, Trevor. I am so sorry."

She took his hand firmly and held tight. After a long awkward moment, he shook off the dark memory and offered a pale smile then finished his beer.

"Shall we invite Beryl and Bill out for an evening?" she said on the walk back to Wild-swallows.

"Say, that's a good idea!" Trevor said. "We've got the car and I'm dying to find out more about Shrewsbury dining. Can you arrange it?"

"I will find us a cozy place to eat, maybe something different—do you like Thai food?"

Trevor smiled. "Lots of Canadians enjoy Thai cuisine, so I'm up for it!"

"There are genuine Thai restaurants in town, believe it or not. Immigrants bring good things, you know!" Brianna said.

Trevor saw how happy she seemed and a feeling began to come over him.

Could I make someone like her happy? Would I be happy if I did?

They turned and entered the inn.

Bright bright stars glittered in the sky as the frost began to settle silently on fields and farms in the broad valley of the Severn.

Chapter Five   In Peril

It was hard to go about your business without someone noticing, or gossiping—especially if you had recently come from some other part of the world.

In a town like Shrewsbury there was some anonymity but in a village like Briar Hill your chances were slim to nil.

The fact was--that Trevor was becoming quite interested in what had transpired at Broadmoor and the mystery of what happened to its owners.

But he was quick to realize that asking questions could get you into deeper water—even if your intentions were innocent and your motives pure.

Any mention of 'Broadmoor Castle' was met with stony silence or outright avoidance.

Trevor knew there had to be people who knew something about it; if there had been a scandal with the brother, they would have stories or some kind of recall.

It should not be necessary to start from zero.
 But whom to ask?

As it turned out, the 'whom' asked *him*.

"You've been wondering what the story is about yon castle in the hills."

It came more as a statement than a question.

"Yes, sir, I was just curious. I am doing research on local history and I wondered…"

"You'd better be careful what you ask around here, sonny me lad," said the old man, who was often to be seen snuggled into a corner of The Root & Branch nursing a pint.

"There's bad blood in this," he went on. "No one knows 'cause no one talks, but I can tell you straight—there's evil afoot and no mistake!"

Trevor ordered and paid for a round of drinks, settling himself into the soft leather bench across from the old man with the penetrating blue eyes beneath thick overgrown brows jutting out like hedges from a weather-beaten face.

A farmer? A retired sailor? It didn't matter. Trevor was hooked.

"I knew Lord Trethewey," he related. "He knew my father in the Navy. He had come home on leave and on occasion dined with us. Marvellous chap--with stories boys love to hear."

"I'm astonished that a lord with his status would even *be* in the war," Trevor said.

"That's what an Englishman is made of, son. Every man does his duty—regardless of class or circumstance. Roger Hardy was no different."

"After the war, men came back to pick up the pieces of their lives. My Dad was engaged when he shipped out of Liverpool and got married the same day he came back! Good thing, too. She was pregnant with me!

Lord Trethewey not long after had himself a lovely bride as well. Some say she was from north Wales. Welsh ladies are real beauties. You should be lookin' over the border if it's a wife you're after."

Trevor grinned and swallowed the mild and flavorful local brew.

"Soon the children came and the village prospered as Shrewsbury became the county seat of commerce once more.

More than just wool, all kinds of goods were traded in and out—carried by train. The old days of river traffic were long gone.

In '41 our little town did not suffer the bombing by the German Luftwaffe that others like Coventry did."

Trevor saw the old man's expression as he drifted off into the past—but not for very long.

"As I was sayin', the Lord and Lady were committed to making the family estate livable.

Can you imagine trying to heat a forty-room castle...all that stone and glass just sucks the heat right out? You'd go bankrupt in a year!

It was rumored that all was not well at Broadmoor, however."

The man's voice dropped a notch and he leaned in toward Trevor, his eyes looking dark in the shadow of his cap.

"Aye, it were *the son*—so said the grocer and his wife that serviced the castle with fresh food each week.
Something about that boy was all wrong. And—temper? He had a streak of the Devil in him.

At any rate, he up and left--and they had peace for a time.
Until one dark night in November—oh, about twenty years ago now. 'twas tragic. Tragic."

Trevor didn't get to hear the next chapter of the Hardy saga as the working men and women came off their shifts and piled into the pub with hearty cries for 'beer' and 'pints'.
To his surprise, the old man excused himself to go to the washroom but did not return.

***

It was Tuesday and rainy in town when Brianna and Trevor entered the law office of

Alfred David Long, Barrister & Solicitor, for advice.

"Good morning, Brianna...Trevor. Ah, I didn't get all your details: are you...husband and wife?"

"Not at all," Brianna said firmly. "Friends."

"Right. Well I had my staff look into a few things for you, and I'm afraid the news isn't good.

First off, the title to the property and the castle remain in the family name. The taxes are being paid and utilities and maintenance are not in arrears. So the county has no issue with its current resident."

"And who would that be?" said Brianna hotly.

"Mr. Rodann Hardy."

Brianna swooned and Trevor seized her before she fell to the floor.

"Get some water!" shouted the lawyer to his assistant.
Brianna came around quickly and was obviously in shock.

"That is my half-brother! How in God's name did he get his grubby hands on our family home?"

"I haven't spoken to his solicitor but my understanding is that the property was vacant and taxes were owing, but since he is technically a family member—he is entitled to reclaim and occupy the land once title has been cleared of any liens and debts.

He has what the law calls a 'color of right' to possession and to do what he chooses to do with it."

"This can't be happening," said Brianna. She looked at Trevor plaintively. "Do something!"

"Then surely Brianna has an equal entitlement to possess and use the property," said Trevor.

"It's not so simple," said Mr. Long.

"If Mr. Hardy claims—and I am sure his solicitor will advance this argument. Brianna has no right of occupation since she is now an adult. She will be considered to have abandoned her claim to Broadmoor by moving away from the estate."

"I did *not* abandon anything—I was forced out by the local child welfare authority and put in the care of my uncle and aunt. As was my sister Beryl!"

"Yes, this is unfortunate. However, the law is clear on this point," said Long.

"Well I am going to march right up there and bang on his door until he lets me in. And once I am there, I am not leaving!" Brianna was flushed and Trevor made her drink more water.

"I should advise you that your brother has no obligation to speak to you or allow you in—unless he wants to sell the property or substantially modify the nature of the property—open a tin mine for example—or destroy the property in a way that diminishes its value."

The lawyer was an experienced and capable attorney and came highly recommended—with a price to match!

The news was indeed bad and Brianna could not settle for hours—not until half a bottle of French Chablis had disappeared down her throat.

"So what happens now, Trev?" she said.

"What happens now is that we find a way to get him out—and *you* back in.

Without breaking any major laws or killing anyone, although I know that has crossed your mind," he said.

"That son-of-a-bitch! Just how did he know my father was planning on going abroad on a diplomatic mission and that my mother would be alone with us girls?

He must have waited until he could spring his trap.

He knew he could play the guilt card with her.

He insinuated—or forced—his way in and gave his sisters the bum's rush.

But what happened to my Mother? Uncle Jeffrey said she had disappeared but gave no details of why and where."

"Then that is another lead for us to follow," said Trevor, making notes. "There are big empty spaces in the overall picture of what is going on here.

I think we need to begin to covertly observe and track the comings and goings at Broadmoor.

I have a strong hunch that there may even be criminal activity taking place within its stone walls—in which case we can involve the authorities and have his little party brought to a sudden and swift end."

***

The nearly fifty-mile drive from Shrewsbury to Birmingham normally took about an hour, plus another three mile jaunt from downtown to Edgbaston where the main campus was situated.

Normally Brianna left from the train station where Trevor would drop her on the three to four days she needed to attend classes or clinic.

Today, he wanted to see if there was any information in the Cadbury Research Library to help him with the parchment or with history of this part of England. It held over two hundred thousand rare books and manuscripts in its archives—plenty of ways to spend the day.

They got off to a quick start and found the straight and relatively level M5 and M6 highways convenient and well-maintained--as motorways in Britain usually are.

Trevor noticed a late model Volvo with tinted windows seemed to be following them. When he tried to slow down or speed up, it matched their pace.
Maybe it was just his imagination, since they were now getting closer to the mystery of Broadmoor Castle and all his feelers were up.

But they couldn't shake the car—or the feeling—that someone was on their trail. Only when they turned off onto the road into the main campus did the car and its occupants speed off.

Birmingham's medical school had a long and illustrious reputation. Founded in 1825, it was now one of the largest medical schools in Europe,

and had fifteen affiliated teaching hospitals in the
West Midlands.

Brianna hoped to intern at one of them. That
was still a long six months off, however.

"Wait for me at Old Joe, Trevor? Around six I
should imagine."

She gave him a quick kiss on the cheek and
sped off in a crowd of laughing and jostling
students hurrying to be on time for morning
classes.

Old Joe, Trevor remembered, was the famous
red brick clock tower—said to be the highest of its
kind anywhere, located prominently on campus
and named for its first chancellor Joseph
Chamberlain—the man who persuaded Queen
Victoria to grant the university a Royal Charter in
1900.

Trevor turned his map over to locate his
destination. There! He strode over to the
commons to grab a cappuccino beforehand.
Dozens of students also apparently agreed that
coffee was a decent way to start the day!

The flash had already gone before he realized
that the attractive young woman behind him was,
in fact, capturing his image on her cellphone.

And just as quickly—she slipped backwards
like a dolphin at sea, and was gone!

He was left with only two possibilities: one, she
had mistaken him for someone else, or two—she

had followed him for the express purpose of getting a photograph of him, for reasons unknown.

The hair on the back of his neck was reacting as the thought of being stalked sank in.

So. We are not alone.

Chapter Six   Family Secrets

"Who was she?"

Brianna was out of breath from the walk to the clock tower to meet him at the agreed time.

"I have no idea. I've never seen her before. She did not say anything to me. Could be an accident, a case of mistaken identity. Weird though."

Trevor exited the lot and returned the way they had come until St. Mary's Church spire could be seen on the hill that announced their arrival in Shrewsbury.
There was no sign of the Volvo, or any other cars behind them.

"Shall we eat in town?" he asked.
"No, not tonight. Beryl expects us and will have prepared dinner. And I don't feel comfortable after dark out on the street. Can we just go home?"

She looked so lovely in the lamplight Trevor decided. Her golden locks framed her face with a beauty that belongs to a Botticelli...he straightened up and pulled his hands down over his face.
He was tired. There was still a twenty to thirty minute drive to the inn called Wildswallows. He

thought he should ask her one of these days how it got its name.

He maneuvered the car onto the sliproad and motorway and turned up the interior heat from the control console.

Autumn was here at last. The sun set earlier and the mist in the valley grew deeper. Like a fluffy blanket of white. Made one sleepy just to look at it.

Trevor splashed warm water in his face and eyes then came downstairs.

"How was yer drive to the big city?" Bill said.

"Hah…just fine. Nice fast road," said Trevor.

"You weren't expecting visitors were ya?" Bill continued.
"No, why?"

"There were a white van parked across and they were taking photographs of the inn. But they didn't get out even when they saw me on the front stoop looking at them.
Gave me the creeps, they did!"

Brianna looked at Trevor but he just shrugged. She went to the window and pulled the blinds down and then the lace curtains together—pinned with a clothes-peg.

Beryl had cooked up a stew of short-ribs with carrot and potato, and soon all was forgotten as the delicious food was eaten.

After dinner Trevor wanted to tell Brianna more about his grandfather—and his own quest in England.
Beryl and Bill retired early as a rule, and watched TV till late in their bedroom off the kitchen at the back of the inn.

They left Trevor the cozy fireplace to pull up to where Brianna a chance to put her feet up on the ottoman to warm at the fire.

"I wanted to tell you something, Brianna. I have something to show you."

Trevor took out the parchment from its leather tube and pulled his wing chair close to the sofa and laid it across her knees.

"What is this strange script? Where did you get this? This reminds me of the warning that was given to me two weeks ago!"

"This was discovered in the library of my own home in Rosedale—a Toronto neighborhood where my family lived for a number of years.

"I was hoping to decipher it or glean some insight into what it means; I know it is Brythonic or what is called P-Celtic. That means it is Welsh or Cornish rather than Scottish or Irish Celtic.

Some of this appears to contain glyphs or symbols—similar to your message, and similar to stone circles and monuments found throughout the British Isles."

"Why is this important right now? I need to find a way to get into that castle!"
Brianna tossed aside the parchment and stood up—back to the fire, glaring at Trevor.

"I have to reclaim something too, Brianna. I didn't come all the way to England to see Wordsworth's 'field of golden daffodils'."

Trevor hastily rolled the document and stowed it in its case, his voice becoming heated also.

"My grandfather was a high member of the Druid Order and had spent years in England during the War doing something that was important to him.
He discovered something along the way that was so incredible he kept it a secret from his wife, his son, and his grandson.
"I want to know what that was--and all I have is this weird document and a strange ritual object

that he obviously wanted to be found by someone in his family after he died.

I might be wrong but I believe I was meant to have these objects and inherit the secret he learned, and the only thing that makes sense to me is to come to the land of his birth—the land of my ancestors—and do my utmost to find out why my family destiny is tied to an ancient Celtic pagan religious tradition."

Brianna sat down and looked steadily at him.

"I am beginning to think that it is more than coincidence that our paths have crossed," she said softly.

"I know you are going to think I'm crazy but I think my father was also vaguely connected with the Druids," Brianna continued.

"He loved to celebrate Nature festivals and took his children to Samhain and Solstice and Beltain celebrations in the South of England, where hundreds of folk would gather. He and Mum would weave wildflowers into our hair."

She turned in the firelight to look at him.

"He once told us a story," she continued.

He said that his great-grandmother was a possibly a priestess in a forgotten band of the Order of Druids.

She had used the castle as a gathering place for performing mystical rites and for study of the ancient Teachings.

Although Dad was an Anglican, he had great regard for the Old Way and I think he tried to reconcile the teachings of Christ with the timeless knowledge of Nature Spirits and Gods and Goddesses of the Celtic people.

For all I know there are lost heirlooms of my family hidden away that will reveal what they knew.
You see--this is *my* destiny, Trevor.

It's not just about the castle and the property and the trust fund that was left to us—but kept hidden.
It's part of *me*! It's who I *am*!
Trevor—we *have to* get inside that castle!"

Trevor poured the dark red wine.
"Then a pledge! *May the powers of Heaven and the blessings of God and Christ be with us in our worthy quest for Truth and Justice. We shall not rest until we have them!*

They both drank deep and together uttered the final word of the prayer: *Amen.*

Chapter Seven   Scared of The Dark

The gravel crunched as vehicles entered and rested in the drive of the outer courtyard.

The fountain was alight with colors as water shot up and fell back in a curtain of rain that floodlights from the rim illuminated.

Burning torches jutted out from holders in the walls along the front and sides of the front of the castle.

Well-dressed people wearing masques were escorted into the massive entryway to the castle itself—behind equally massive oaken doors with iron bands and rivets adding strength and weight that could prevent an army from gaining access to the great hall inside.

Broadmoor was hosting a masquerade.

Service vehicles parked around the side where the entrance to the kitchens and scullery could be found. Men were unloading crates of specialty foods, desserts, and vast quantities of liquor and wine in a seemingly endless parade--in and out.

"This is a hell of a party!" whispered Trevor.
"Who *are* these people?" Brianna replied.

They had parked in a clearing off a service road that had been set fifty or so yards off the main entry road—the one they had used last time.

The gate here was much smaller and had swung open to allow deliveries and service people who were apparently hired to clean up after the festivities. Trucks and vans had the names of local businesses that no doubt profited from whatever the master of the castle had arranged.

Like faint shadows, Brianna and Trevor snuck in to the castle grounds.

Getting inside the building without an invitation or without knowing a soul would not be possible. In any case, they were here to spy—not join the fun.

"With those masks on, we are not going to get a good idea of who is wearing them," said Trevor.

"Whoever they are, they have money," said Brianna with a snooty tone.
"Jaguars, Benzes, Bentleys—why would they drive way out in the countryside like this? For privacy?"

"My guess is they want to do whatever it is they do away from nosy people and public places," said Trevor.

The last of the guests arrived and the big iron gates clanged shut--closed by a security guard in uniform.

It was just half past nine and the moon was not even up yet.

"What now?" said Brianna.

"You know the castle inside out, right?

Let's find a place where we might get a glimpse of what's going on inside. Someplace where we won't be seen," said Trevor, zipping his jacket and pulling a black wool cap over his ears and head.

Brianna did the same. She made sure she had not worn earrings or anything shiny that would be picked up in the light.

"Around here," she waved. There is a passageway between the main building and the wing that stretches back into the oldest part of the castle. This is where the library and the chapel used to be."

Trevor felt better in near-total darkness along the east wall of the central edifice. The stones were cold and damp as they felt their way along the high wall toward the one tiny lamp burning inside the passageway.

There was a narrow door there--mullioned with antique glass panes in a lozenge pattern— down at the end that was nearest the main structure. It was open!

"Do we go in?" said Brianna. "If we are caught, there could be unpleasant consequences."

"I don't think we have a choice. We need to find out what Broadmoor is really being used for and who exactly is in charge of that," said Trevor.
"I want to see if your brother is really the big *kahuna* here," he added.
"I brought my GoPro, and I'm going to get something worthwhile out of it.
If we get caught, we can try to make a run for it. I know some martial arts tricks."

Trevor was smiling but they both could feel their pulse starting to pound in their throats.

***

The noise was almost physical.

The pounding music and manic laughter— voices carried up--with the heat and scent of sweat and smoke from below, up into the halls and into the wide landings and alcoves many feet above--all of which lay in shadow.

"They are topless!" breathed Brianna.

Couples danced and held each other, glistening bodies in the firelight and torchlight, naked above the waist—and with very little clothing on their lower half.

They were delirious in their wild gestures and frenzied kissing and petting, so much so that Brianna had to turn away.

"This is like a Roman orgy!" Trevor exclaimed.

There was an ornate stage with a large throne upon which was sitting a young man with dark hair and a glittering metal crown, dressed somewhat more than the boisterous crowd.

In fact he was dressed like a knight of old— chain mail over leather, resting his weight in part on a large medieval sword that gleamed and—like the crown-- spoke of leadership and authority.

Brianna gasped.

"It's him! It's Rodann—my brother!"

As if some psychic link, some resonance in the blood was aroused, the man on the throne twisted and looked right up at them!

They were well enough concealed, and dressed
all in black, so that they were sure he could not
actually see them.

But those eyes! They held a mighty power that
would humble anyone if their gaze fell upon them.

"I am afraid, I am afraid of here," said Brianna.
Take me from here, Trevor, I beg you!"

She tugged on his shirt and pulled his arm like a
frightened child would.

They found their way back to the passage with
the small glass door and stepped out into the
chilly fog that had crept in to conceal their retreat.

The dashboard clock showed half-past
midnight as they carefully eased their car back
down the muddy ruts of the service road.

No one followed them and the stillness of the
night was a sharp contrast to the pandemonium
inside Broadmoor Castle.
There was no car to be seen on the road that
led out of the black hills and down to the friendly
glow of the village of Briar Hill.

Both of them went straight to their rooms.

The moon shone in the window and across the
sill of Trevor's room. He lay on his back looking at
the ceiling.

He had not even slipped out of his clothes and
when the morning came his shirt felt clammy and
smelled of body odor. He tossed it on the chair
and went for a very hot shower.

   ***

"Now I see where he gets the money to
maintain his residence at Broadmoor," said
Trevor.
They were on the M5 to Birmingham and each
nursing a hot coffee.

"How can he get away with it?" said Brianna.

"He obviously has good lawyers who let him
stretch the law to his own benefit.
It is an axiom of British law that a man's home
is his castle; property is sacred to an Englishman.

So the law permits almost any activity to be
undertaken on your own property; and is very
strict about interference with that right," said
Trevor.
"The hoary law of trespass is a good example.
You so much as set foot on another man's land
and the law provides penalties in both civil and
criminal law to protect the right to be utterly free
of any invasion or interference with the use of that
land," he said.

"So you're saying that having wild parties with alcohol and drug use are acceptable uses of private property?" Brianna said with an edge in her voice.

"Legally—yes. Morally—questionable. It seems clear that some wealthy people like to participate in these—Bacchinalia—and they no doubt would have connections to powerful people," continued Trevor.

"And the masquerade motif allows them to be more of less unrecognizable during the celebrations," said Brianna.

"Exactly. It even adds to the excitement knowing you could have a close encounter with anyone whom you choose and yet remain anonymous."

"Sexual fantasy, in other words."

"That's a powerful motivator—especially coupled with the opportunity to make fantasy become reality."

"Have they no shame? They were doing it right there, in the Great Hall—in *my* family home!"

"This must cause you great pain to see your former residence turned into a Roman spectacle of debauchery and lust."

"I thought I was in pain knowing that I have been literally shut out by Rodann and his collection of sycophants, but this—this is ten times worse!"

"We will put a stop to this Brianna. I don't know how yet—but we will find a way. We will!"

Trevor's fist came down so hard on the dash that his coffee splashed all over his trousers and shoes.

Instinctively he glanced up into the mirror to see if that Volvo was following them, but the road was only full of trucks and commuter buses.

Soon the university campus came into view and they parked, leaving at least a twenty-minute walk for Brianna.

She suddenly took hold of both his hands and looked up in his eyes.

"I can't do this without you, Trevor!"
She found his closeness and strength so reassuring and she rested her head on his chest for a moment.

"You won't have to, Brianna."
He pulled her body to him--one hand cupping the back of her head, the fine blonde filaments of

her hair protected from the chilly wind in that moment of warmth and perfect stillness.

****

Cadbury Research Library had an old section and a new section.

It had undergone extensive renovation ten years ago and large windows now threw light into airy open spaces near the ceiling, and onto little nooks here and there where comfortable loveseats and chairs had been thoughtfully placed.

But the books Trevor was looking for were in the cramped dark little aisles in the old building.

This was the rare books section. You were required to wear white gloves before handling any manuscripts or other material.

You were permitted no food or drink and CCTV made sure this rule was enforced.

As it turned out, for years lovers had found its cozy recesses a nice place to be intimate but cameras put a stop to that.

The online catalog had arranged the material by both subject matter and time of publication.

Nevertheless, it was quite a challenge to find pre-Roman Celtic sources since few records were put in writing at all. Rome's great gift to the

Britons was to introduce Latin literature and essays from its great writers like Marcus Aurelius and Pliny, and histories including that of Julius Caesar who conquered Britain in 54 B.C.

Trevor knew that the Celts of Cornwall and Wales would resist the Romans—as they would resist the Saxons five centuries later.

The suppression of Druids by the Romans would drive them to the west and there the trail grows cold.

Fifteen hundred years later a Druid revival is taking place in Britain as hurried urbanites search for a meaning to their existence and turn to the Old Religion.

Did it bear any resemblance to the original? he wondered.

And what was it Grandfather had found that changed him into a reclusive hermit with virtually no outside contact for the last five years of his life?

Trevor held the key in his hand--but what door would it open?

He decided that the esoteric side of the Old Religion—Magic--might hold some of the answers.

The parchment might well be a magical formula, or a procedure, that gives distinct powers to its owner. The *dorje* was a tool to exert power of a certain kind. Did it confer the gift of prophecy? Or geomancy? Or of destruction?

His grandfather seemed to be taking Druid art and practice to its limits—and maybe beyond.

It is there that the mystery really begins--and Trevor really hoped that his grandfather had not strayed into the darkness of the Left Hand Path— the path of black magic.

He *had* to decode the parchment to know for sure what the truth was—and he had to do it *now!*

***

After dinner, Trevor and Brianna went to the sitting room and drew close to the fireplace.
The light and heat and comforting crackle of the logs made a perfect end to a busy, stressful day.

"Before I tell you what I did today, I wanted to ask you something," Trevor started.

Brianna pulled her Welsh woolen shawl around her shoulders and put her feet up.
"Yes, Trevor? You want to know if I have got a placement near home, so you don't have to drive so far?"
She was in a playful mood.

"Well, yes, I do want to know that, Dr. Hardy, but I also have been puzzled about why a lovely girl like you is not married yet?"

"Well, why aren't *you* married, Professor Gower? At near forty—and an eligible bachelor."

She went on teasing in a half-serious way.

"I have been trying to focus so much on my career that I forgot to even ask you if you have a girlfriend back in Canada.
Or perhaps a secret wife!"

"Oh *that's* what you've been thinking, is it?"
Trevor was grinning as he leaned into the light of the fire to poke a smoldering log into the flame.

"You can't blame me for that!" she replied.

"Oh no—on the contrary; I'm delighted that you are thinking about me at all!"

"Well, I'm not. It's just that sometimes I wonder what will happen after all this is over— one way or the other.
I mean, when your year in England is up and you will go back to your life in Toronto and your job and...whatever."

"Honestly Brianna—I haven't thought that far ahead. All I want to do is figure out this damned parchment. The answer is probably staring me in the face but I still don't see it."

"Don't worry, I know you will solve it, Trevor."

Without hesitation, she placed her hand on his arm—only to withdraw shyly.

"I didn't think any of this would happen during my year away," said Trevor.

"I may as well tell you that seeing you again was one of the principal reasons I decided to take time off.
To come to England. To...spend time with you.
Why? Ask the stars! I never told you about the dream—did I?"

"What dream?" she said.

"My first night in Cambridge. I saw two things that made a deep impression on me. One was I saw the lady—yes, *that* lady! The Lady in White!
And then a beautiful woman with golden hair appeared and I knew I loved her at that moment."

Brianna was fidgeting.

"Well, when I met you after my lecture, when your friends came up to me, I couldn't help but think that you were that girl—in my dream.

And I got such a rush of feeling I wasn't sure I could stand being there in your company.

Since then I have been struggling with the dilemma of the dream-girl compared to the real-life girl."
He looked at her.

"Is any of this making any sense?" said Trevor.

"Well I'm glad to know I am like your dream girl--only I am trying to organize my life!
Perhaps one day marriage and family will be at the center of it. I hope so."

"You think I'm playing with you?" Trevor's body stiffened and he shifted back in the chair.

"I don't know what to think, Trevor. I don't know your heart.
And anyway, you didn't answer my question. Is there someone in your life back home?"

"No. I haven't even looked. I had a bad experience a long time ago. I'll tell you about it some other time."

"Look. I really appreciate your help, Trevor and I really enjoy your company. So can we just leave it at that for now? Please?"

Trevor nodded and a little smile snuck up from somewhere inside.

"I am glad to be here, Dr. Hardy. I am entirely at your service," he said with mock politeness.

"Good. Let's get some sleep. God knows what tomorrow might toss at us! Good night, Trevor."

Chapter Eight   Haunted

"Stars, hide your fires; let not light see my dark and deep desires."
                    Shakespeare

The story of Robert Hardy—known now as Rodann—begins with a secret, a shadow that lay buried in his family's past.

It is said that Lady Trethewey—when she was just plain Estelle Lupin—came from London--but that little else was known of her.

But the birth records for Middlesex County, City of London, District of Knightsbridge showed that a certain E. Lupin gave birth to a male child, seven and one-half pounds, on such-and-such a date.

The local hospital records also show that a Miss Estelle Lupin gave birth and then disappeared almost before the ink of her signature was dry.
    No father's name was given.

Some years later, the signature of Estelle Lupin appeared on the Shrewsbury marriage register beside that of one Roger Hardy, Lord Trethewey of Strathmore, only son of a local nobleman whose family were well-known over many years in the Midlands.

It would be highly unlikely for a bastard son who had been abandoned twenty-one years ago in London to ever appear at his own mother's doorstep in the north of the country—but that is exactly what happened.

It was a dark and stormy night. The chill of November hurled sleet and hail at the windows of Broadmoor Castle and the wind shrieked like the very soul of Evil.

Near the great gate a group was gathered in the gloom. From beneath his hood its leader spoke.

"Drug them—both of them, then bind and take them to the place near the bridge.
The children are to be hooded and bound and brought to Abbey Grange fifteen miles north. You have your instructions.
Make sure Trent receives them. Take care not to show your faces. Return here and wait for me."

Gloved fists pounded on the oaken doors until they spilled light onto the wet stones at the entryway. Cries could be heard.
Then the entrance was shut and tires spun in the gravel and soon all was quiet again—but for the infernal wind.

Not long after, the castle was closed up and gates were locked. No light shone from its windows. No voices of children were heard.

And so it remained for the longest time.
Broadmoor Castle lay hidden in its lair of dark spruce and pine, far from civilization, cloaked in mystery.

No one suspected that the castle had new tenants—and if they had, they would have fled in fright!

Grim men with swords and stern countenance would occasionally emerge in fair weather to practice their fighting arts or strange rituals among the trees in the grounds surrounded by the strong thick walls of granite and sandstone.

The Dark Ages had returned to Broadmoor.

The few brave souls who passed on the highway might dare to approach the iron gates that were the only opening—to try to see *something*.

Some brought back tales of a ghostly lady in white-- walking on the parapets forth and back as if condemned to spend her days in utter misery, searching for--but not finding--peace.

In time, the shadow of Broadmoor grew so that locals spoke only rarely of it, and in hushed tones.

Darkness had engulfed it.

Trevor—by luck—had been introduced to a much older professor at the university in Birmingham who was regarded as somewhat of an expert in lost languages and alphabets.

The parchment seemed to fascinate him, and the two pored over it in an anteroom of the Cadbury Library on the principal campus.

"Look here," the professor said. "This doesn't make any sense if we try to translate it directly. It's a cipher, a code. Facts are buried within a lexigraphical puzzle; it's a tossed salad of words and meanings. I understand by it has bedeviled you for so long."

Professor Burnaby wiped his glasses with a handkerchief he pulled from his blazer pocket.

"Why would your grandfather have made it so difficult to read, I wonder."

"I assume it is secret esoteric knowledge that is not to be given to the uninitiated or casual observer," said Trevor matter-of-factly.

"He intended that I should have it, however. There must be a strong reason *why*.

I believe he wanted me to know something he had discovered—a secret of such immense significance that it might wreak havoc if it were publicly disclosed."

"Good Heavens! Do you really think so?" said the old man.

"Put it all in context, Professor. It was hidden away with this strange object of Tibetan or Indian origin, where no one but me would ever be likely to find it, and once I did—he knew I would relentlessly pursue its translation and discern its significance."

"We must tread carefully then," Burnaby said.
"Can you leave it with me for a day or two? I need to consult some old documents--I cannot remember where they have been filed but which may throw light on our quest."

"I have made color copies on good quality paper and I shall leave you one of those, if you don't mind. The original I keep with me at all times."
"Of course, Trevor, I completely understand. Come by on Thursday week and I will tell you what I have found out."

"Thank you, Professor Burnaby."

Driving home, Trevor was deep in thought. Brianna wanted to talk.

"I have been offered a position at Shrewsbury Medical Centre as an intern. That means I can complete my training and qualify to write my certification exams in two years—instead of three. Plus, I don't have to go to Birmingham several times a week.

"I can sleep more, save some money, and enjoy life a little more.

Are you listening, Trevor?"

"Yes, that's wonderful, darling." The word slipped out before he had even realized it.

"You can sleep a little longer, save the train fare and have more time for yourself," he said.

"That's what I just said! You silly man! Lost in thought, are you? What did you find out at Cadbury?"

Trevor summarized his visit with the old professor.

"I'm afraid ciphers were not part of my medical training," said Brianna.

"I know there is a way to get at this. Did you ever hear of 'frequency analysis'?"

"Sounds like some statistics thing," said Brianna.

"The principle is simple really: look at the word size and the frequency with which a certain letter or symbol appears. Once you get a sense of what each means, translate it and bingo!—there's the message."

"Well, tonight is unavailable. We are having a glass of wine by the fire after supper, and you are snuggling up with me on the sofa."

Brianna leaned toward the driver's side and gave him a quick kiss on the cheek.

"Well, if you insist Doctor Hardy," he smiled. "Absolutely!" she said. "Doctor's orders!"

***

Trevor checked his personal e-mail. His work account was always choked with spam, and student appeals to his good nature, to review a grade or accept a late assignment or some such.
He would avoid his Earlsdale maibox as much as possible—he was on holiday!

One new message from an old buddy from University of Toronto days.
Fred Taylor was now a prominent lawyer in the city but occasionally they would go to a local bar for a drink.
Fred was a complete nut on Rome and the Roman Empire. He obsessed on all the details of which emperor replaced which other emperor,

who led the army in this or that battle—anything Roman!

So not surprisingly, the e-mail message was short—but Trevor knew it was an invite to go grab a couple of beers.

It simply said: "Hail, Caesar!"

To which Trevor replied: "Homo quid facit?" which translates as "What's going on, man?"

Fred got back to him and that gave Trevor a chance to explain what he was doing in England again and why he wasn't available.

Later that day, Trevor had a sudden epiphany!

Julius Caesar had conquered Europe and invaded England.

Later research showed that his messages to troops and, of course, to Rome were often encoded so they could not be read by his enemies—of which there were many!

The so-called Caesar Cipher is not used in steganography or data security today—it is too simple to decode.

But maybe, just maybe Trevor's grandfather could have used it—or one like it—to create the cryptic communication on the parchment.

"Brianna? Can I bug you for a minute? I need your fine mind."

Brianna was helping her sister in the kitchen dress and marinate two partridges to be cooked for their supper tonight.

"Yes, my dear? What can I help you with?"
Since she had taken a residency at the hospital in town, Brianna was much happier and it showed in her speech and manner.

She had always been kind and courteous, but she was positively bubbling with energy these days.

"I want to show you an idea that came to me. It's about the cipher.
There's a famous code that Julius Caesar used that might get me closer to the answer I'm seeking.
Let me show you how it works.
Let's take a word like 'apple'. If we encode it using Caesar's Cipher it will now read as 'dssoh' and be meaningless to the casual reader."

"Ok. So take my name 'Brianna'. In code that would read 'EULDQQD'. Am I right?"

"Correct. You've got it! Now let's lay out the parchment and figure out what these forty-seven words might say."

"But I've got to help Beryl finish the dinner preparations," she protested.

"Oh, I'm sorry. I pulled you away, didn't I? Let me bash away at it—you go back to help her," Trevor said.

Brianna gave him a brief, ever-so-fleeting kiss -- but this time on the lips.
Then she slipped out of the room and could be heard singing a snatch of song from the English popstar George Michael.

Three sentences start with the letter 'L'. Code-breakers know that the most commonly used letters in the English language are 'e, a, o, i, n and t'.

Let me assume that 'L' equals 'I'.
Trevor was on a roll.
The first two sentences—if I can call them that— start with the same two words: 'L KDYH...L KDYH'.

So that means: 'I'...what?? If I go back three letters I get 'H' for a K and 'A' for a D and 'V' for Y and 'E' for H. "I have..."

Trevor started to pace nervously.
The code was unravelling right before his eyes.

The fourth word in the first two lines was three letters long.
English--like all European languages—uses a part of speech called an 'article' to identify a noun.
Articles are either 'a' or 'the'.

What if this word is 'the'? Now it reads: "I have____the_____!" The third word must be a verbal complement to the auxiliary verb 'to have'.

It is five letters: IRXQG. Decoding this reads: 'found'. "I have found the____"...what? It must be important or Grandfather would not have written it this way.

Trevor then went through the whole thing replacing encoded letter with translations, and bit by bit he realized this might be how it could be solved.

'VHFUHW' was the last word of the first sentence.
SECRET! That's it—'I have found the secret!'

Trevor now understood that the punctuation was important as well. *But what secret is it talking about?*
His train of thought was interrupted.

"Dinner, Trevor," said Beryl in a cheerful voice steaming into the room with an enormous covered platter.

Trevor rolled up the parchment and stowed it in his room, then washed up and came down to eat.

Chapter Nine   Trent's Story

Abbey Grange is a charming estate of about two hundred acres located southeast of Shrewsbury, not far from the old Benedictine abbey which gave it its name.

The Severn meanders lazily across the heartland of England in the Midlands. All around are farms and fields full of grain and cattle, each with its portion of woods which supplied lumber and firewood in times past.

It came into the Hardy family generations ago as a grant from the Crown for services rendered to His Majesty in the war with France in the Hundred Years' War.

Jeffrey Hardy thus inherited the title Earl of Trent along with the magnificent residence and lands. Lord Trent married a highborn lady Jodie of Locksley in time, but they were unable to have children and this was a grave disappointment for them.

Jeffrey was well-liked in the district and his cows—managed by excellent local dairymen—produced good milk and even better cheese.

His wealth derived not from this however; he had copper mining interests in far-flung countries which continued to be highly lucrative.

The Countess of Trent loved to entertain and on certain days of the year would host lavish parties with guests invited from their social circle among the nobility.

Moreover, she had stables and kept thoroughbred horses that were used as sires and mares for some of England's finest equine specimens.

It was common for countrywomen to ride and raise horses—the Queen herself was very much attached to horses and related sports. Her husband Prince Philip of Macedon had been a serious polo enthusiast in his day.

Unlike his cousin Roger Hardy, Jeffrey had not served in the military, and his inclination toward business distinguished the two men from each other.

Roger, too, had inherited title and land— including the impressive Broadmoor Castle up in the hills of west Shropshire.

But despite their slight differences the two were close and Roger's daughters were only too pleased to be invited for a horseback ride or to attend events where the Trent stable would present its finest in breed.

Indeed, they were doted upon by the Countess who no doubt regarded them as family and had arranged rooms and living quarters in the Grange specially for them.

How ironic, then, that one terrible night some years ago, strangers appeared--with the girls bound and covered with blankets--pounding on their front door at Abbey Grange.

"Are ye the Master Trent?" one scowled roughly, looking at Jeffrey and Jodie with hooded eyes.
Jeffrey said: "Yes" then, "What the devil do you want?" but the men's only answer was to haul the girls out of the back of the vehicle and fling them at their feet.
The house staff quickly took them inside to the warmth and shelter of the manor, while the frightful men sped off in a tradesmen's van— never to be seen again.

"Oh my darlings, what has happened?" The Countess was beside herself with worry.
"Help us Auntie, help us! Evil men came and took Mummy and Daddy, then others took us. It was all so sudden!"
And they burst into a flood of tears and grief.

They were taken upstairs to their quarters to wash and find clean dry clothing.

The Earl called the police.
"No, I didn't get the number plate—they were gone just like that!
No, I have no idea *who* they are or how they got our girls.
I am very much afraid that foul play has occurred at Broadmoor and I beseech you to send your men to investigate at once!
I have reason to believe that the other residents have been kidnapped and are being held against their will.
If I get more information, I will telephone at once.
Yes, thank you!"

But the police had no news the next day--nor the next--nor the next after that.

Lord and Lady Trethewey could not be found.

The *Chronicle* gave few details, since none were known.
The newspaper did report that the girls had been released by their captors to The Earl and Countess of Trent who were relations anyway and this brought relief to the townspeople who knew and wanted to know everyone's business.

But no hint of who or why emerged--and the case in police files grew cold.

"Why ain't there a ransom demand or some such?" asked the constable in charge.

"Don't make sense," said PC Willett.

"We've naught from the bindings on the girls," said the Sergeant. "Can't get a print off fabric."

"Who's been let out of prison lately that has a history of violence?" said Willett.

"Don't they *all*?" said the Sergeant.

"Aye. Well maybe something will turn up," said the constable in charge of the investigation.

And that was that.

***

The two girls were still children: Brianna was eight and Beryl was fifteen when this calamity swept them away like a tempest at sea.

They knew little of their half-brother, Rodann. He had been driven out two years earlier by both his stepfather and his mother.

The girls could only speculate about what had led to this—perhaps his misbehavior, perhaps his violent disposition, which they had already witnessed as young children.

Now all the adults had vanished and left them with Lord Trent and away from their rightful home at Broadmoor.

"When'll we see Mum again?" said Brianna. Being the younger, she had little experience of life to give context or meaning to what had happened.

"Dunno," said Beryl. "Auntie has said nothing. P'raps she won't want to speak over Uncle Jeff."

"How long will we have to stay here, Beryl?" Brianna was insistent.

"Dunno that either. Least we'll get to ride the horses," she said trying deliberately to put on a brave face for her little sister.

"What's happened to Dad. What's happened to our family?" Brianna was bereft and cried herself to sleep on the long winter nights.

"I've spoken with the solicitors," said Jeffrey, "and they are confident that the trust and its assets are secure. They've consented to make me trustee until such time as Roger returns to his estate and puts his affairs in order."

"Can't Estelle do it?" said Jodie.

"Unfortunately, the terms of the trust grant authority only to the male of the clan.

This is not Roger's doing.

It is a clause that has been traditionally included in the family inheritance since the 17th Century. English law regards wills and trusts to have legal weight regardless of their antiquity.

This is why I—not you—have the responsibility for managing the fund on behalf of the girls. They are of the opinion that the bastard Robert Hardy has no legal claim to the money.

I am very much afraid that he might hold Roger and Estelle to ransom in order to get a share of the family wealth," Jeffrey explained.

"That's bloody extortion!" said Jodie hotly.

"Yes! That's exactly what it is!" he said.

"Well can't we do something?" she said.

"First we have to find him," said Jeffrey. "Once we find him, we can find out what he's done with Lord and Lady Trethewey.

I can't help but think that the local constabulary could be doing more to find them and bring this criminal lot to justice!"

"And who's to say we aren't next, Jeffrey? We are part of the Hardy extended family and have access to all kinds of money—including that trust fund.
We also have custody of the two remaining legitimate heirs to that money and to Broadmoor. I am concerned that our safety and the safety of the girls may be in question."

"I hadn't thought of that," Jeffrey admitted. "I should've. I will speak to my solicitor and make security arrangements for Abbey Grange.
I'm still in shock that those blokes could just pull up at the door and toss our nieces into the gravel like sacks of potatoes.

No—you're right, Jodie. I will have men at the gate standing guard as soon as I can arrange it."

The wind was picking up and carried a blast of snow and sleet across the fields and stables, right up to the Grange main buildings.

The Countess of Trent wrapped herself tightly in her favorite cashmere shawl and hurried up the staircase to check on the girls.

***

"I want you to meet them, Trevor.
They were like parents to us after...after it
happened." Brianna's voice fell away.

"Yes, I would like that. I would also like to ask
your Uncle Jeffrey a few questions that have been
lingering in my mind."
"You're not to blame him in any way," said
Brianna firmly.

"No. Why would I do that?" said Trevor.

"Well, just in case you think they had anything
to do with this," Brianna said.

Trevor held her long coat for her as she slipped
her arms in.
"Don't wait up, Beryl!" she called to the kitchen.

"No worries, love," replied Bill. "We'll be
snoring shortly after you've gone."

Bill had a sense of humor, Trevor thought. The
English wit is one of the characteristics of Brits
that appealed to him.

They arrived at Abbey Grange, only to be met
by two sturdy security men who asked them what
their business was at the house before admitting
them.

"This started when Aunt Jodie began to worry more and more about what danger we were all in," said Brianna.

"Well, you *were* in danger," said Trevor.

"Nothing's changed," said Brianna. "Let's get out of this rain, shall we?"

The Earl of Trent was of course twenty years older and where there was still hair was now white.

He hugged Brianna and warmly shook Trevor's outstretched hand.

"Oh darling!" said the countess descending the stairs. "It's been so long since we've seen you!"

They held the embrace, and then the countess said: "Who is this handsome fellow you've brought along?"

Trevor took her hand and bowed awkwardly.

"I am honoured Countess to make your acquaintance."

"Oh. Jodie—please," she said.

"This is my friend Trevor Gower from Canada, Aunt Jodie. He is here to do some research and has landed up being my partner in crime."

Jodie's brow arched. "Oh? Crime?"

"We are seriously planning to find a way to get Broadmoor back from Rodann," she said.

"I thought that was a lost cause," Jodie said. "He has some powerful friends and clever solicitors to protect his little kingdom."

"I can't wait anymore," exclaimed Brianna. "I will be thirty years old in a year and a half. I want to marry and have the life I once had—and was cheated out of!"

"Then have it—but forget about Broadmoor.
Creepy old castle with too many rooms," said Jodie. "You'd need a staff of twenty to manage it."
Find yourself a cozy little house in Shrewsbury with all the conveniences.
They've got some darling shops along High Street. Why don't we go shopping sometime—just you and I?"

"Drink?" said Jeffrey, pouring himself a Scotch.
"Do you have wine? Brianna loves a glass and sometimes the wines here are not half bad," said Trevor.

"Where in Canada do you hail from?" said Jeffrey, pulling the cork on a bottle of burgundy.

"Toronto. I teach college there. Snobby private school for girls."

"And what do snobby girls learn these days?" asked Jodie.

"There is a standard provincial curriculum that happens to include history and social science. I've been at Earlsdale for thirteen years. I still think I can make a difference in the world, so teaching is a job I believe in."
Trevor clinked glasses.
"Cheers, and thanks for your warm welcome," Trevor said.

"We'll hope you'll stay for a while," said Jodie with a broad smile. "Don't we, Brianna?"

Brianna flushed pink then hid behind her glass as she tipped it and asked Trevor for a refill.

"I'm afraid I've mucked up Trevor's whole plan to study in England," she confessed.

"What exactly are you studying, Trevor," asked the Earl.
"Celtic traditions and ancient beliefs," said Trevor. "I've got an ancestral link to the West Country and perhaps some connection to the Old Religion—the Druids."

"Well you certainly came to the right place for *that*," said the Earl.

"We've got Druids and all sorts here and stories that go back many centuries. Have you heard of the crop circles?"

"Yes!" said Trevor. "I wanted to spend some time in Wiltshire where they seem to have a spate of crop circles every summer. Fascinating and mysterious!"

"You never told me that!" said Brianna, teasing.

"You never asked," said Trevor with a smile.

"I think it only fair to tell you that anyone who goes poking about Broadmoor today is being foolish," Jodie continued.
"Jeff and I have friends who have friends who have become acquainted with the goings-on up there. Not fit for polite company."

"We had a look ourselves," said Trevor. "Got past the gate one evening and had a chance to sneak in a side door. Not our cup of tea," he said dryly.

"That is quite a risky undertaking," said Jeff. "There are rumors of young people who have gone to spy and not been seen again.
I've made inquiries through friends about whether the police know, and have been met with embarrassed silence," he said.

"You mustn't put yourselves in danger, Brianna," said Jodie.

"Is there anything you might know that could help us gain some ground in the struggle?" asked Trevor.

"I still think it goes back to what happened to Roger and Estelle," said Jeff.

"There's dirty business in all this.

If they had been kidnapped and possibly harmed, there must be some kind of evidence trail that the police seem too inept to pursue.

I should've hired a detective but frankly I was afraid to. If I pulled the tail of the tiger, it might go badly with us—especially having the girls here."

Jeffrey stood up and walked to the sideboard and poured another glass of whisky and took a long pull.

"I'm sorry we can't be more help," he said. "I can offer you some financial backing for your investigation, however, if that'll be helpful."

"Thank you—thank you both!" said Brianna, throwing herself into their arms.

"You gave me a wonderful childhood and I know I speak for Beryl when I say we cannot express our gratitude. I love you, Auntie Jodie—Uncle Jeff. We will be in touch!"

Trevor shook hands and they slipped out into the night, arriving somewhat past midnight to a quiet house.

Chapter Ten   Dr. Hardy, I Presume?

Brianna admitted to herself that it would take some getting used to--to think of herself as 'Doctor' Hardy.

But in St. Mary's Hospital she was going to hear her name quite a bit over the P.A. system.

As an Accident and Emergency Room physician, she would get all kinds of situations—from sick children to seniors with stroke symptoms or injuries from falls.

The work was physically and emotionally demanding and her shifts were sometimes doubled if it was a bad night out there.

Hospital workers need strong backs and a good pair of shoes.

They also need a good night's sleep and an occasional proper meal. These were hard to come by when things got hectic at St. Mary's.

Brianna was the kind of person that made friends easily—even when she wasn't looking for a social contact. Her cheerful energy and natural approachability drew both staff and patients to her.

One such person was Gemma Watkins, a recent hire from Scotland, who was assigned nursing duties in Accident & Emergency and worked many of the same shifts that Brianna did.

"I'm shattered," she said as she put on the kettle. "And I don't do half the work you do!" she said to Brianna.

"Remember when you did your training and dreamed of the day you would be working in a real hospital?" said Brianna.

"Gawd, that was ages ago," replied Gemma.

"You don't smoke do ya?" she said. "I'm ducking out for a fag."

When she returned the tea was made and the girls sat sipping as the ward began to settle for the night.

"Tell us about your situation, then. Do y' have a boyfriend?" Gemma was nothing if not direct.

"No, not exactly. Let's call him a 'friend' and leave it at that," said Brianna with a smile.

"How is he in bed?" said Gemma mischievously.

"Like I said—we're just friends. Haven't got to that stage yet."

"Aye, but you will, right? At some point?" said Gemma.

"That depends on a lot of things," Brianna said.

That nudged Brianna to start thinking over the next few days about something other than triage.

Near the top of the list was whether Trevor would stay in England, or return to his job in Toronto—once his year away was up.

Brianna realized that they had seldom talked about personal things, like a couple would—and should.

Beryl had slyly teased her on occasion about him. Of course she was concerned about her little sister and wanted nothing more than for her to be happy.

But Brianna had to admit to herself that she did want marriage and kids and a marvelous man to share it with. She just had been too busy to devote time to making it a reality.

With her 29th birthday coming in December she knew that the time was coming to make the big decision.
But she had not even had time to test the market—there had been some possibles at the

university medical school but they were quickly snapped up as graduation day approached.

Shrewsbury was a small pond and most of the men were either married, not available, or not interesting.

In any case, she had been distracted by the whole Broadmoor thing.

Is there some hidden significance in the fact that Trevor came back to England? He said he came to see me; is that true? Or even realistic? He seems like a romantic dreamer to even think such things.

The conversation in her head was amping up after her little chat with Gemma.

Later that week, on break, Brianna turned the conversation the other way, asking Gemma about the men—or man—in her life.

"Yeah, I had a fella back in Dundee. Oil rig worker, he was. I was too young to know what I wanted, and you can guess what *he* wanted.
Every spare minute he wasn't out on the job," she said.

"I told him I wanted to finish school and settle down, but he weren't much interested in long-term plans. Typical.

So when I passed my Board exams and got my license, I decided to chuck the whole thing and come south.

Don't ask me how I landed up here. Honestly, I think I took the first decent position I saw in the adverts.
Could ha' done worse, though. It's not half bad here in Shrewsbury and I've got a little flat in a newer townhouse that lets me bike to work most days."

Brianna had growing respect for Gemma's gutsiness and frank manner.

"So we should go out for a pint and see what the local men are about," said Brianna.

"You're on! At the week-end," said Gemma.

    ***

Late one night—it was a Thursday she recalled—a young man with serious head injuries from a motorcycle crash was in A & E and Brianna was the doctor on duty.

The patient was intubated and on a glucose drip lying on a gurney in the hall.

"BP stable, vitals holding," said the nurse.

"Let's take a look at that head wound," Brianna said. "Help me turn him."

It was bad. He had lacerations on his neck and hands, and what looked like a skull fracture and torn scalp.

"Get him to X-ray immediately! Tell the radiologist to call me on my extension. Tell him I want to know if there is bleeding inside the skull."

A burly attendant wheeled the gurney swiftly down the hall toward Radiology.
Brianna spoke to the Admissions nurse.

"Who brought him in?"
"Ambulance, Dr. Hardy. A cop in uniform in tow."
"What did he present with?"
"Significant blood loss with depressed vital signs, not conscious and not responding well."

"We have a name? Contact?"

"No ID. Cop said his bike was hit by a lorry and the lorry driver has been charged for driving drunk."
"Where did this happen?" Brianna was making notes.
"South on A49 toward Briar Hill and the RAF base."
"He wasn't wearing a helmet," added the nurse.

"He'll be lucky if this is not his last motorcycle ride," said Dr. Hardy. "What was he thinking?"

Brianna had no choice but to wait for the results of the X-ray scan so she slipped into the kitchen for a cup of tea.

Gemma breezed in and greeted her.

"'member that big red-headed fella I was chatting up the other night?" she said.
"Well he's gone and asked me out for next week-end! How do you like that?"

Brianna gave her a quick hug.

"Well *that's* nice," she said. "You're off to a great start, Gemma! New job--maybe a new man. I'm excited for you!"

"Yeah! Things are looking up. Me Mum always said "Tomorrow's a new day!".

"Where's your Mum? Back home?"

"Nope. She passed away not long after Dad did. Congestive heart failure."

"Oh I'm sorry, Gemma. That must've been such a shock," said Brianna.

"I miss her, Brianna, I really do! She was my rock. She handled everything. Now I'm alone."

"Dr. Hardy? Dr. McPhee wants you on Line Two," said the nurse.

"Excuse me. We'll chat later," said Brianna heading to her office.

"There's good news and bad news," said the radiologist. "The good news is he is regaining consciousness and the x-ray shows no subdural hematoma. There is a small area of fracture but I expect it will heal up with no major complications."

"And the bad news?" said Brianna.

"He seems to be delirious and rambles on about Camelot and King Arthur and that he is a part of it and has to get back. Makes zero sense.
Anyway, I'm releasing him to Psychiatry if you want to speak with him."

Brianna did.

Given he was found in the vicinity of Broadmoor Castle and maybe he knows about what is really going on there, Brianna figured that he might have something valuable to share that would help her and Trevor in their mission.

"How are we feeling?" said Dr. Hardy to the young man in the bed, looking at the scalp sutures.

"I have to go back, Miss. Can you get me out of here?"

He struggled to rise but fell back onto the mattress—partly because the tubes and wires made it difficult to just up and go.

"What's your name?"

"Terran. My last name is Welsh and you won't be able to pronounce it anyway."

"What do you know about Rodann and the castle?"

Brianna was betting that—in his foggy state of mind—Terran would let slip information that could not be obtained any other way.

And she was right.

"We're building a new Camelot. We're resurrecting the Knights of the Round Table and renewing the quest for the Grail," he stated.

"Here, drink some water," said Brianna handing him a glass. She knew he was dehydrated and she really wanted him to be able to speak clearly.

"Rodann says we can restore the rightful king to his throne by forming The Order and committing to expanding its influence to all parts

of England, Scotland and Wales—where King
Arthur fought his battles against the Saxons and
led the Celtic people to victory."

"So all of you 'knights' live and train at the
castle?"
"There are twelve—plus Rodann—and there
are others. Amanda--who claims to be a witch
who has some magical something-or-other that
can help. I think she just screws Rodann really.

There are 'servants', he calls them. Some quite
young."

"What about the parties? Who are those people
and what have they to do with your Camelot?"
asked Brianna.

"They fund us—they are the moneybags that
Rodann exploits by having these unrestrained
events where he lays on the booze and coke—lets
'em do pretty much whatever they want."

"What's your general opinion of your leader—
of Rodann?"

"He's powerful. He knows how to get people to
do what he wants.
He punishes those who disobey. That's why I
have to get back. He will notice I'm not present
and will punish me if he thinks I am speaking with

any outsiders. He has a torture chamber in the dungeon. I am afraid!"

The nurse on the Psych ward came in and suggested that the patient get some rest now.

Brianna had lots of information to digest. *Trevor must hear this* she thought.

***

"Jesus!" said Trevor. "This place is really nasty!"

"So what's our next move?" said Brianna.

"I don't know if it will work, but I think we should go to the police and tell them what we know," he said.

"If he gets busted, that will make it a whole lot easier to get our legal claim on the table," Trevor said.

"Let me get dressed. Tell Beryl to put out some lunch for us. I have a feeling it's going to be a long day."

"Mr. Gower? May I call you 'Trevor'? And Dr. Hardy? Thank you. Please sit down."

The Assistant Chief of The Shrewsbury Constabulary had agreed to hear their story; he had a secretary in attendance.

"Now let's hear your observations first, Dr. Hardy, since you are evidently a legitimate heir to the estate of Lord Trethewey."

The Vice-Chief—as the front desk cop called him, was cool and detached but professional. He was a man of about fifty, overweight and out of shape, but neatly dressed in a grey suit, sporting a regulation moustache.

Trevor watched his reactions as Brianna outlined what she knew--without giving too much detail about how she knew it.
For now, the cop didn't ask.

"And what do you expect the Shrewsbury Police to do here, Dr. Hardy?"

"I want to regain possession of my family property and in order to do that—I want my brother removed."

"That would be a matter for the solicitors I would imagine," said the Vice-Chief smoothly.

"Well can't you go investigate, and find out if these rumors are true? Find out if there is criminal activity going on?"

Brianna's voice rose a notch.

"We have had no complaints," said the Vice-Chief. "If there were illicit activities we surely would have heard something by now."

He went on.

"I am quite sure that the tenants of Broadmoor Castle are within their rights and within the law," he asserted.

"It might also interest you to know that the Chief and I had been invited to a gathering some time back and I can assure you nothing untoward or of a criminal nature occurred.

I fully understand your desire to contest the issue with your brother, but I can see no grounds for any further involvement of law enforcement."

The Vice-Chief stood up to announce that the interview was over and he strode out the room, leaving a duty officer to show them to the front lobby of the station.

"How do you like that?" Brianna said. "He just gave us the boot—like he didn't want to listen to us or give us any credibility at all!"

"But he admitted they had been there—him and the Chief.

If we find out that they were there when certain things like drugs or child abuse were happening, then they are in deep shit," Trevor said.

Chapter Eleven   Moonsilver

Trevor had got word of a local psychic who identified herself as a 'witch' and so Trevor wanted to speak with her for two reasons.

Firstly, he wanted to know her take on the *dorje*--which was essentially a crystal ball in a bronze clasp. Crystal balls were the province of seers and psychics.

Secondly, he wanted to know if she could cast some light on the castle and its bizarre rituals. Trevor was versed in ancient religion but not very well acquainted with the actual rites and what they were used for.
Perhaps the woman who called herself 'Moonsilver' could be of assistance.

Brianna liked her right away.

Moonsilver was in her forties and worked out of a cottage not far from Briar Hill on a functioning farm that belonged to her family. She was a 'local'.

"Let me say at the outset that whatever I say to you should be examined by your own good sense and judgement.

I don't have magical powers and I don't change frogs into princes."

Brianna asked, "Were you born with this ability—to *see things* I mean?"

"I am fortunate to have a lineage from the women in my family which Granny called 'The Second Sight'. As a girl, I had pictures come into my mind about things that happened in the future or would happen to certain people—some I knew, but most I didn't."

Trevor was fascinated too. He noted the variety of 'tools' as she called them scattered around the room--from Tarot cards to crystal wands and a huge quartz crystal ball sitting on a special pad.

She had a wall chart of the *chakras*—Yoga teaches that we must awaken these power centers in the spine through powerful meditation techniques, often called Kundalini Yoga.

"Is this....*teachable*?" asked Brianna innocently.

"I think the techniques of meditation or of Remote Viewing can be taught. To me, the key is awakening one's own spiritual Consciousness. That is the goal of Yoga, of Druidism and esoteric practices of all kinds.

In the Middle Ages, alchemists struggled to transform Lead into Gold, but only the adepts—the real initiates in the secret occult lore—knew that Lead referred to the body of flesh and Gold to the Spirit body that all humans possess."

"What is 'Remote Viewing'?" Trevor said.

"This is the more modern term for 'clairvoyance'—an old occult word meaning literally 'seeing at a distance'.
It is believed that we can awaken a sixth sense that allows us to 'see' and 'know' things that are otherwise unavailable to us because of barriers of Space and Time.

"Can you do that?" he asked.

Silvermoon laughed softly.

"Oh, Trevor—*you* can do it, Brianna can do it.

Think of it as part of a software suite that your Mind comes equipped with at birth.
If you don't know it's there—you will never use it. Well, you *could* have an accidental awakening or vision of some kind but these are rare.

I promise you, if you develop your awareness through regular practice of some technique such as yoga meditation, you *will* switch on these--

'powers' if you like, as I believe we were *meant to*."

"Now, let's get down to the business at hand; what has brought you here today?"

Brianna was the first to speak.

"My brother fancies himself as some sort of Druid mage or sorcerer. God knows what tricks he has learned about the occult but he has become a powerful magician in his own right.

The worst of it is that he has displaced his parents and his sisters—me! from our family home and installed some kind of secret order he calls The Order of Wolfbane in the castle and they are up to some nefarious plot to resurrect the lost days of Camelot and King Arthur.

But I don't think he sees himself as King Arthur—or even a reincarnation of him."

"Ah, good! You are familiar with the concept of reincarnation, I see. Tell me more," said Moonsilver.

"He exerts a mysterious hold on his followers and maybe practicing black magic for all I know. I want you to suss him out, see if you can discern what powers he wields and how Trevor and I can find a way to defeat him."

"Beginning to sound like Lord of the Rings," said Trevor drily.

"I see." Moonsilver looked thoughtful. "You are talking about Broadmoor Castle, aren't you?"

"Yes!" said Brianna emphatically. "I am the rightful owner inasmuch as my parents have...disappeared and not been seen again."

Brianna didn't want to say 'died'. It was too painful to contemplate and was unlucky.

"Let me begin with the Tarot," Moonsilver said.

She shuffled and passed the cards to Brianna.

"Cut them three times and place them in one pile on the table," Moonsilver said.

Brianna did as she was instructed.

Moonsilver spread the deck—composed of 72 cards in two categories: Major and Minor Arcana—and selected three and placed them face up toward Brianna.

"Queen of Wands. That is *you*. A brave and noble lady who has lots of energy and has a goal to achieve something important."

Brianna leaned in a bit and Trevor shifted his chair so their bodies were touching. She briefly looked up into his face as if questioning or seeking his approval. He looked at her tenderly.

"Justice. Major Arcana. Major force at work in the situation. It says that the situation will result in a fair and just outcome and the right decision will be made.
I'm going to go out on a limb here and suggest that the law and the justice system favor you, Brianna. You are the aggrieved party, after all. I think this card gives hope that all will be well."

Brianna tugged on Trevor and he put his arm around her shoulders and pulled her into his chest.

"The Tower. This card says a violent and unexpected event or condition will turn everything upside down.

The Tower represents the Unexpected, the lightning bolt that strikes—just like the image on the card shows—and topples the tower and hurls the king to the ground."

"Does that mean it could end in disaster?" said Brianna with a tremulous voice.

"It means that we can't predict for sure what the ending will be. All I can say for sure is that

The Tower always predicts some serious shit is going to happen!"

Brianna whispered something to Trevor and he kissed her on her forehead and continued to hold her to him.

"How about the crystal ball?" asked Trevor.
"I didn't know they were anything more than toys or paperweights," he said.

"Crystals have been used since time immemorial by those who might be regarded as shamans or wizards or—as in my case—*witches*."

"What *is* a witch really? I never met a witch and frankly never wanted to," Trevor said.

"You know the history of the medieval Church and their position on witchcraft, I assume.
You strike me as a highly educated fellow, so I won't reiterate how women were persecuted for their innocent pagan practices as herbalists and healers in times past.
Witches today are Earth goddesses, healers and diviners who seek to attune themselves—and their community—to the Nature forces which infuse this planet.
Our belief is—and always has been—that there are natural laws and energies that are present in natural and unspoiled places that can awaken

spirit awareness both in humans and in the Earth itself."

"So magic wells and stone circles and caves, you mean?"

"Exactly. The Earth is a bundle of energies and vibrations that can help—or harm—human beings.
When I say 'harm' I mean they can be misused or improperly handled.
Just like electricity. Don't respect the power and use it wisely—it can kill you!"

"You've heard of 'ley lines' then?" said Trevor.

"Of course. The Old Ones and of course the Druids knew of these lines of power that link up certain places on the landscape and give heightened awareness and power to those who knows their secret."

"So again—like cables and wires that carry electrical power across the country," offered Brianna.
"Just so," said Moonsilver.

"I wonder if Broadmoor Castle is situated on such a ley line?" Brianna wondered.

"If it *is* then that would give enhanced power to any rituals or ceremonies conducted on its grounds," confirmed Moonsilver.

"You started to talk about crystals," said Trevor. "May I show you something?"

From his pack he took out a small bag containing a piece of cloth; inside the cloth was the *dorje.*
He held it out for Moonsilver, but she would not take it.

"I am careful not handle objects like these," she said. "They can contain energies of Darkness or dissonance that can burn you—like a bare wire.

May we immerse it in salt water briefly while we talk? And I will say a prayer of Purification over it," she said.

"Let me say more about why crystals are often used.
They have a unique ability to focus energy— and when I say 'energy' I mean 'intent' or thought," she cautioned.

"You must realize that Thought is *Energy.*

Science shows that the brain is an electrical generator and that our nervous system uses electrical signals to transmit messages to and from the brain.

It stands to reason that thoughts--which are focused, concentrated--concentrate energy, and that energy can be stored. Crystals are storage devices," Moonsilver said.

"That is interesting!" said Trevor.
"The heart of a computer is a silicon chip and silicon is the main mineral in quartz crystal!
So what we're saying here is that crystal balls act on a similar principle!"

"You are getting the picture, Trevor. Crystal balls were supposed to store thoughts and the energy of the thought depended on the *intention*.

Thoughts of healing and peace and harmony were called White Magic; thoughts of control and harm were called Black Magic.

I think that at some point the Church fathers realized that witches and wizards and the like had a kind of spiritual technology that was beyond their understanding and so they suppressed it," she said.

The sun was setting in a blaze of orange and pink in the windows. A last gleam of light came through the window and struck his crystal *dorje*—just as it had done months ago in his office.

It was as if it were a *sign*, he was thinking.

"Can you show us how you use your big crystal?" said Brianna.

Moonsilver sat quietly upright and began to breathe in long slow rhythm—her eyes closed and hands resting upon her lap.

At length, she turned to left her ball onto the table and began to study it, look at it—unblinking and intensely focused.

"I will verbalize aloud my thoughts so you know what I am trying to do here," she said.

"First I said a prayer so God will direct this procedure to our highest and greatest Good.

Now I will send a thought into the depths of the crystal, asking for clarity about what Brianna can—or should do.

The room grew still and all eyes were on the transparent globe as if it would light up like a computer screen.
"I see darkness. I see evil intent. I see danger. This person is wearing a cloak of shadows. His purpose I do not know—but his methods are crooked. This is the Left Hand Path. He is powerful. Stay away!"

Moonsilver broke her concentration and lifted her ball into the tank of salt water and removed and dried Trevor's.

"I am sorry if I alarmed you. It was more than I expected when I tuned into his energies.

Brianna, you would be advised to leave this alone. You are out of your depth here.

This is not just a case of a group of thugs gone wrong.

There are astral energies that the Bible calls 'demonic' at work here.

No, no, no! Stay as far from Broadmoor as you can!"

Brianna asked if there were prayers or spells for protection.

Moonsilver said "Ask Christ to bless and protect you." This is the Supreme Power in both worlds, she said.

Trevor quietly put his crystal into its case and they put on their coats, thanking her.

"I don't know how it will turn out but there is something good to come, Brianna. Just be patient.

Good night!"

The frost was gleaming in the moonlight as they made their way to the car.

"I don't now what to think now, Trevor," Brianna admitted.

"Let's get home and have some food and we can chat around the fire after," he said.

After this unusual experience with Moonsilver the Witch, he wanted nothing more than to get where it was warmer and lighter and safe.

***

"We can't give up because a so-called witch says 'oogah-boogah'," Trevor said over breakfast.

"And since the police are not going to help, we need to go back to our two private detectives—*us!*"

"I have a job now, Trevor and it's taking a lot of my time and energy. I can't be lurking about at night with a camera--spying on my brother."

Brianna was having coffee—a sure sign that she had a hard day ahead of her.

"Yes, of course, and I don't expect you to. But we can't stop now—we're making progress; I know it." Trevor was insistent.

"I have to get inside that castle and catch them in the act—whatever 'act' that might be. If we can prove there is criminal wrongdoing we can take something substantial to the police and force them out of their indifference."

"Maybe Moonsilver is right. Maybe it is too dangerous at this point. Maybe we should wait for Rodann or some of his men to make a mistake, get careless and draw attention to themselves," Brianna said.

"And maybe that won't happen. They've been doing this for years and getting away with it, Brianna.

Here's my idea: they have these parties from time to time and it is probably when they are most vulnerable. Traffic comes and goes and all the attention is focused on the guests having a good time. The locked gates are wide open.

Rodann will need to announce these dates, but we are not on his e-mail list. But if we can have eyes on the highway that runs up there through our little village here, we might be able to determine when it's going to happen.

He needs food and drink and other supplies delivered; all we have to do is note when the traffic noticeably increases going that direction, and we can make the assumption.

That RAF station, I'm guessing, is supplied from the south, coming up into the hills that way on the A49--and not through Briar Hill."

"Who's going to be your spy in Briar Hill, then?"

"Oh, don't worry. I have just the man in mind," replied Trevor.

***

The Root & Branch had been serving local ale since 1838 and some of its patrons looked like they had been there since opening day.

Public houses (or *pubs*) were more like a home than home for certain men and the warm dim interior was always full of smiles and friendly folk from local villages and towns.

All local pubs had a similar style—old oak timber ceilings and plaster walls, bric-a-brac on every windowsill, sturdy oaken pillars and comfortable benches and tables that made you feel more welcome than any modern tavern or coffeehouse did.

Trevor looked for him in his usual spot in the corner--away from the bar and hubbub.

"I'm sorry, I didn't get your name last time," said Trevor, sitting himself down across from him.

"Niall Watson," said the weather-beaten old man. "And yours?"

"Trevor Gower."

"American?"

"No, Canadian. Taking a year away from teaching to explore by English roots."

"Aye, you look like the scholarly type. Smooth hands and clean clothes. Gower you said?"

"Yes. My Grandfather was a business magnate in Bristol—J. Rossili Gower. He was in the import-export trade."

The man continued to study Trevor.

"My father and mother were both Christian missionaries and declined a life of comfort in favor of service," Trevor went on.

"And where is your family now?" said old Watson.

"All dead sir, I'm afraid," said Trevor.

"Aye. So what is it you would be researching in the West of England then?"

"My area of expertise is old Celtic beliefs and traditions. Particularly the Old Religion—Druids."

The old man took a long pull at his ale and smoothed the foam out of his moustache and beard.

He looked more directly at Trevor now as if scrutinizing him to get more insight into this young Canadian.

"So that'd be why you're interested in yon castle then?"

"Aye…I mean 'yes'." Trevor had slipped into the vernacular without realizing he was doing it.

"Which brings me to what I'm here for, Mr. Watson."

"Say on," said the old man. "And it's Captain Watson if ye don't mind. Royal Navy. Class of '41."

"As you seem to know," continued Trevor, "there's odd and sinister happenings up at Broadmoor. I've made some inquiries with the police in town but they have little to offer.

I'm going to have to do some legwork myself and pay them a visit to see…to observe what they might be up to."

"I've seen ye going about with the Hardy girl," said the captain.

"Yes. I'm…helping her with some legal matters with regard to regaining possession of the castle from the rascal that currently occupies it."

"And you want my help?"

"Here's the thing, sir. You are usually here at the Root & Branch and being close to the main road you must notice…"

The old man cut him off to complete the thought.

"...the kind of road traffic that goes up into the hills and so I can be a pair of eyes whilst ye go about your business."

"Yes! They open their gates from time to time when there is an event and that is the time I want to slip inside and document whatever I can," admitted Trevor.

"Well, ye're either completely daft, or the bravest young fool I ever met," said Capt. Watson, starting on his third pint.

"Captain! I don't see what choice I have!"

"You must have some kind of powerful strong affection for this Hardy girl to stick yer neck out this far," the old man said.

"I never thought of it that way—I suppose there's some truth in that.
In my mind, I'm helping justice be served. The world is full of bullies and thugs—someone has to stand up to them. Just like my parents did."

"You said they were missionaries. Did they run into trouble?"

"They died defending their school and the children in some stinking civil war in Africa, perpetrated by a corrupt military regime.

None at the school had guns or grenades—and I doubt they would have known how to use them."

"It's all coming into focus now," said the old man.

"I'll make you a deal," said Trevor. "I'll cover your bar tab for a month if you would just keep watch over the highway and text me when you notice something."
"That's mighty kind of you, Trevor. Only I don't 'text'; I don't have a cell phone. No need for it."

"Can you use the pub phone? I'm sure they won't mind. Just give me a quick heads-up; I'll write down my number. Here." Trevor passed the slip of paper to the captain.
"I'll speak to the owner before I go. Doesn't matter what time you call—I'd really appreciate it."
"Have ye considered the consequences if that lot catch ye up at their hideout?
Billy Barrigar went poking around up there one time and they beat the living jesus outta him and threw him in the road. That—after burning him with irons.
Police didna believe him as he was a no-count street punk with no business being up there. He said he was just having a look about and they said they could charge him with trespass on top of it all."
"I'll be careful, Capt. Watson."

"Aye. Ye do that," the old man said.

On his way out Trevor stopped at the bar for a word. He passed the owner several banknotes of a respectable denomination and left quietly.

The call came sooner than expected. Brianna was at the hospital working until late.

Trevor had to guess exactly on which night the event would occur.

He asked Capt. Watson what he had seen--and based on that--Trevor was sure it would be on the weekend.

Tonight it was all suppliers and caterers who would be doing the setup--which would take hours—if not days. He had time to prepare.

He would drop into the fitness club in town and run some laps, and do some bench presses to ensure his muscles were strong for the coming adventure.

Then pick up Brianna and get home before midnight and wolf down the food Beryl always leaves out for them.

Mentally Trevor ran through his plan and what clothing they would wear, and equipment like flashlights, GoPro, even a survival knife. He felt like a commando on a raid. In a sense, they really were. This could be the breakthrough they needed. If luck would be on their side.

Chapter Twelve   Captives

When Capt. Watson called again, Trevor knew the game was on. Fancy cars and limos snaked up into the hills as the sun slipped behind the mountains of Cambria--of Wales.

"Are you sure you want to do this?"

This time it was Trevor doing the asking.

"I care very much about you, Brianna. I would never forgive myself if you got hurt."

He had his hands on her arms with a look of genuine concern.
He wasn't smiling and his forehead was wrinkled. *He's cute when he's serious*, Brianna mused.

"We've come this far, Trevor."
"We have to see it through. No matter what comes," she said.

"Okay. I just want you to know that I... really..."
He choked his words.
"...respect you."

He looked down, fumbling to zip up his black hoodie and help her into hers.

It was the night of the Blood Moon—an unusual partial eclipse that threw a dusky shade of red across the brightness of its surface.

They parked a bit further and away from either of the gates in a small clearing beside the highway.

Trevor surprised her when he threw an army-style tarpaulin over the car, so that it could be camouflaged from searching eyes.

Their feet crunched on leaves and branches as they came upon the southern gate—the ones service vehicles always used and which were wide open for these few festive days.

Late guests were still arriving.

A police van and cruiser were pulling in and Trevor and Brianna ducked behind another truck.

"That's…"

"Yes, I know," said Trevor. "The Chief of Police in Shrewsbury.
But notice he's not in uniform. He's rather over-dressed to be on duty…so he's *not* on duty. He's come for the party!"

"Looks like he brought the Vice-Chief along for the fun," said Brianna sarcastically. "Ironic—his name. *Vice*-Chief."

"Stop it!" said Trevor obviously amused.

"Let's wait till they are inside and we shall see if our little side door is still unlocked."

"Wait! Trevor! It's the ghost again! See her?"

"I see it. Why does she appear just when we are here?" he said.

"I'm sure she walks about when the moon is full and maybe at other times. Why is she here? I don't remember a ghost when I was a girl. Should we try to get up there?"

"No. Let's focus on our mission. We need to get solid proof that illegal activities are happening here and go to the authorities with it.

Given that the two top police officers are present as participants—that could be a problem. I will take it to Scotland Yard then."

"Did you...?"
"Of course. I waited until their faces were fully illuminated and I shot twenty seconds of video," Trevor said softly.
"They are going to have a hard time explaining why they are here. I hope to get even more com-promising footage inside.
Let's try the back door."

"Wait, Trevor. There's something on the stones. It's a lady's bracelet."

Brianna was so overcome she had to sit.

"Trevor! This belonged to my Mother! There are thirteen Burmese rubies set in sterling silver. She never took it off.

Why is it *here* of all places?"

"Good question. Did it fall off when they were abducted years ago? Did someone else find it only to lose it again in this very spot?

And isn't it a coincidence that we are here under a full moon and it's sitting there—as if we were meant to find it?"

"It fits me," she said. "Help me with the clasp— it's a little stiff."

The noisy event had begun and Trevor was thinking that might work *for* them—or *against* them. No one will hear them--but they cannot hear if someone is tailing them, either.

"If there are children here against their will, maybe we can find one who will talk to us on camera," Trevor suggested.

"Maybe we will run into that guy I treated in the A&E at the hospital. What was his name? Terran!"

"I don't plan to be in here very long. Let's just get some kind of evidence—then get the hell out!"

They were inside now, stealthily moving toward the inner portion of the castle where the Great Hall was situated, and the corridors that led off to other areas were found.

Trevor was just raising his camera for a zoom shot when a strong hand gripped and spun him around.
"What the fuck are you doing?" said the security guard.

"Oh just enjoying a breather. Quite a party, isn't it?"
Trevor was trying to be calm. He gave Brianna a look so she played along with him.

"You don't look like you're a guest, mate."

"This is actually our outfit. We are going to be actors in the performance later on," Trevor continued, trying to bluff his way out of this.

"Alright. I'll take your word for it. But if you make any trouble, you'll be fucking sorry!"

"Sure. Don't worry. It's all good."
Trevor smiled and Brianna did the same— although her knees were knocking and her teeth were chattering.

"Let's stick with the plan. We will be out of here soon. We have to go down one of the staircases where we are unlikely to be seen."

Trevor took her hand and together they slipped down into the bowels of Broadmoor Castle.

Tonight there were drums—big booming tribal drums and torchlights burning everywhere.

Maybe they have themes—and tonight's theme is Jungle Fever, Trevor was thinking as they glided along the wall, trying to stay away from the railing where they might be seen.

Many attendees were indeed in tropical attire and costumes like grass skirts and necklaces of bone and shell. Some were drinking from vessels made to look like human skulls.

What caught Brianna's attention was the crazed expression on their faces.

"They are all high on something," she whispered into Trevor's ear. "The druggies that come in to the A&E all night all have that glazed look that comes from amphetamines or angel dust or cocaine. These people are stoned out of their mind!"

"See if you can spot anyone underage," said Trevor.

"I see several boys serving the guests drinks; I see two twin girls in bathing attire carrying food and dishes to and from some booths that have been set up at the back of the Hall.
Their bodies have been rubbed with oil to make them glisten in the firelight.
Oh my God—one is nude and lying on a stone slab in the center ring. She can't be more than fourteen! I don't want to watch, Trevor!"

Brianna buried her face in his chest and clung to him.
"They are bleeding her; they have cut her wrists and arms and are draining her blood into a goblet. Don't look!"

It was a ghastly sight! Rodann was lifting the cup of blood to his lips with both hands and then passed it to particular people who were apparently chosen and seated close by the stone.

He lifted his arms and shouted: "Drink from the Cup of Life! Hail to the Goddess!"

This made Brianna turn and tremble with fright and loathing.
Trevor had the camera running the whole time.

"Come on. We've seen enough."

He led Brianna down a darkened hall to where other passages crossed it.

"Which way?" she said.

"I'm not sure. We didn't come this way," Trevor said. "There must be more than one way out of this place. Can you remember any exits from this part of the castle?"

"I was just a child. It was all too big. Let's try this stair down. There will be places where the hired staff enter and exit there. Down near the kitchens."

The two hurried now, sensing danger closing in, knowing the price of being caught.

Ordinary fluorescent lights were burning in this section where guests would not wander and voice of servants could be heard not far away.

Footsteps could be heard but it was difficult to tell if they were approaching or going in another direction.

They didn't have to wait long to find out.

"Stop right there!" a rough male voice said.

"We're lost," said Trevor.

"Let's see the mark."

Trevor and Brianna looked at each other.
What mark is he talking about?

"Let me see your arm." The burly guard pulled up Brianna's left sleeve and looked grimly at her.

He did the same to Trevor, then said: "You are not authorized to be at this event.

All official guests have a tattoo—a mark with a full moon bracketed with two crescent moons. The Mark of the Goddess.

You must come with me."

He shoved them forward toward another staircase leading down.
Brianna had never been in this part of the castle either.
But it didn't take long for them to realize he was taking them to the dungeon.

They were prisoners of The Order of Wolfbane!

Chapter Thirteen   Wolfbane

The dungeon in any castle is a horrible place; this one was no exception.

The original structure was built in the 12th Century by the Norman invaders to subdue the Welsh resistance.

Like other spectacular castles in Wales itself, it had turrets and massive stone walls topped by guard posts and crenellated walkways that could see an enemy half a mile away.

Inside were halls and a library and chapel on the main floor, kitchens and servant quarters on the lower level with access to a courtyard and what was originally stables.

The deepest level had a keep with dungeon and storage rooms where the treasury and the armory had been located.

In 1825, it had been renovated--with a wing added which had windows and bright rooms and gardens with a whole range of flowering plants and healing and culinary herbs.

Later, a fountain was added because the previous lord had married an Italian beauty who lamented the grey weather and needed a symbol of sunny Tuscany.

In the 20th century, electricity came to Broadmoor—and proper plumbing. The grounds were modified to permit motorized traffic and fences made of brick faced with stone were erected culminating at the great front gate—which was really two huge iron gates that mirrored each other and made Broadmoor impenetrable to outsiders.

Lord Trethewey had spared no cost in maintaining his stately residence. Many of the living areas had been insulated and covered with drywall and a heating system with two forced air furnaces had made this cold stone fortress quite livable.

He had left the Great Hall as the centerpiece with its vast roof and columns arching up into peaks of architecture as fine as any in Europe.

But the dungeon was original—cold, damp, dark and dismal.
Originally, prisoners were tortured or chained here, while others slept on filthy pallets of straw. Spider-webs festooned the corners and rats had chewed on the wooden benches and even the wooden doors.

With virtually no light except what leaked in through the cracks of the door from the corridor outside, it was a prison of perpetual darkness.

Trevor used his cell phone to cast light on its grim interior.

"It won't work," he said. "There is no signal down here."

"I'm so cold," Brianna said.

All they had was the clothes on their backs—which were lightweight polyester and hardly designed for dungeon residents.

"We just have to wait for them to come, and then make a break for it," said Trevor.

He sat on an old mattress that had been flung on the flagstones. There were several of them.

He snuggled Brianna--his arm around her shoulders, as they both knew that the only warmth here was of their own bodies.

"I'm too cold and scared to cry," said Brianna—her voice forlorn and tearful.

"He will come for us," said Trevor. "Once he knows—he will come. Be strong."

She felt his strength—in his arms and in his voice. It complemented her weakness—like light to shadow. Like yang to yin. Together they were a whole, a fleeting thought told her.

Then another thought came. *Maybe we belong together. Maybe this is what this is all about. This is our destiny—to be together, to have each other forever.*

Brianna must have fallen asleep from sheer exhaustion, so when the creak and groan of the door swinging open came, it jolted her awake.

"On your feet," said a huge man lifting her roughly and pushing them both blinking and coughing into the hall and up the same stairs by which they had come.

The Great Hall stood empty—although a large round table with leather seating for thirteen had been situated in its center.

Without the noise and confusion, they could see much better that this room was decorated with banners and weapons and tapestries with battle scenes. There was a glass cabinet to one side with a shiny silver goblet and other objects such as silver daggers and bowls.

They were being taken to the very center of New Camelot.

The guards had sheathed their swords now and when they entered, they bowed deeply to the man sitting on a throne on the raised dais.

He was dressed differently—he wore no chainmail or armor of any kind. He had a tunic of red cloth and a leather jacket and leggings, ending in knee-high soft leather boots crisscrossed with iron chains.

His cloak was scarlet and was pinned with a huge onyx brooch.

He was handsome in his own way—clean-shaven, long dark hair and good proportions. He looked like a knight from the olden days.

"Well, Sister," he boomed, "We meet at last."

Rodann stood to receive the prisoners and stepped down to greet them.

He did not embrace his sister nor offer a hand of friendship to her companion.

However, he ordered food and wine to be brought by servants who were no more than children, and they were seated at a great oaken table.

"You should have told me you were eager to visit—I would have prepared a better welcome that the one you received," Rodann said with a sneer and an ironic tone.

"You have no right..." Brianna began.

"Silence!" His voice struck the ears like thunder.

"It is *you* who has plotted and spied and
shown me disrespect. I have treated you as any
trespasser or thief.
    I *could* leave you in the dungeon for the rats
to gnaw your bones if I choose.
    Or turn you over to the police to be charged
with break & enter, or trespass, or mischief.
    Then they could put you in a slightly more
comfortable dungeon--to await sentencing."

Rodann continued.

"I am the Master here, and my word is The
Law. This castle is the home of the New
Camelot and I represent the True King.
Eat, drink—and I shall explain!

Since Alfred the Great of Wessex led the
Saxons to victory in the British Isles over the
native Celts and Roman laggards, the British
royal family has continued for fourteen
hundred years by placing an imposter—a
usurper—on the throne.

The Normans invaded from France in 1066
and replaced the Saxons with their own
lineage: The House of Normandy. William the
Conqueror had two sons and so the first King
Henry came to power.

The Plantagenet union of Wessex and
Normany led to Edward IV and was joined to

the House of York--which produced Richard III
and King Henry VIII.

After the Stuarts placed Catholic Scots on
the throne under James I and Charles I, the
German royal lines again became entwined
through the House of Hanover--and the Kings
named George came to power in London.

Eventually the Saxe-Coburg & Gotha line
from Germany through Prince Albert--who
married Queen Victoria--gave rise to the
present House of Windsor—and Elizabeth II.

But all of this is wrong!" said Rodann,
slamming his fist into the table.

"The true monarch should have been
descended from Arthur—the legendary Celtic
warrior and king, victorious in battles
throughout England, hero to his people.
His stronghold of Camelot united the native
Britons and gave them a kingdom of their own.

Through cunning, and tragic misfortune,
greedy Saxons and murderous Vikings—
followed by Norman invaders--supplanted the
Celtic race and seized their lawful entitlement
to the Crown and Throne of England."
Rodann's voice thundered.

"Our own heritage as Britons was destroyed by Europeans taking our lands and crushing our people.

Our Old Religion was denied us from Roman times, and suppressed by order of the Church— another European invention that was driven down our throats!

"But no more, fair sister! With my foot standing here--in this place, this Broadmoor Castle--I will rally our people to restore Justice and Righteousness to the Celtic race whose blood runs in our veins!"

He was on his feet shouting now, and the room began to fill with the others—knights of the New Round Table—the Order of Wolfbane.

"We will purify this nation—starting again with the bloodline of Destiny that has been denied us until now.

Rise, oh ye Knights, and pledge allegiance to Camelot, to The Round Table, and our King—to Arthur!!"

Rodann's voice rose to a demented shriek!

And the Twelve shouted from one throat: "Arthur! King of the Britons!" and thrust their great broadswords toward the center of their Round Table where a goblet and a rose had been reverently placed.

The Great Hall reverberated with the sound.
Birds in the vast ceiling fled their nests with
a rush of wings and metal rang upon metal.
Then all was suddenly still as the passion of
that moment ebbed, and the blades were
sheathed once more.

"And where do I fit into all this, brother?"
Brianna spoke bravely, rising to her feet and
facing him directly.

"What is your plan for *me*?"

"Join us! Help us keep the bloodline pure!
Be my Guinevere, and together we shall rule
and our children shall occupy the throne of this
land for all time to come!"

Trevor and Brianna were stunned, but the
man's eyes glittered with madness and his voice
cracked with uncontrolled glee.
Rodann was insane but none of those here
would know or be able to see that. Naïve but
desperately loyal.

Brianna wasn't finished.

"Do you really think that your crazy rituals—
drinking the blood of innocent children you have
enslaved will help restore your King?"

"Slaves? They offer themselves to me, to
Camelot. I am protecting the children nobody
wants—orphans, street urchins, drug addicts who
prostitute their bodies for a meal.
      I give meaning to their lives.
      I teach them the way to redemption by teaching
them the most important lesson of all—to serve!"

      It was Trevor's turn to speak.

      "You are a megalomaniac--like all dictators and
despots in history.
      You see yourself as a savior—but you are not.
      You are not a hero.
      You are warped and deluded and you are evil--
in every sense of that word."

      "Seize these ingrates!" cried Rodann. "Throw
them in the dungeon!"
      Strong arms pulled them roughly, but Brianna
had one last question for the deranged leader of
New Camelot.
      One that would pierce like an arrow.

      "What have you done with Mum and Dad?
      What have you done, Rodann?"

      Brianna shouted at the top of her voice with
every ounce of rage and pain that she had kept
inside all these years.

For a moment, it was Rodann's turn to be stunned and he fell back from the force.

Then he replied.

"They abandoned us!"

With that, he ran screaming from the hall--into the shadows that ran deep into the castle.

The dungeon doors crashed shut once more—leaving Brianna and Trevor in filth, fear and darkness.

***

Evening came—or what felt like evening.

A young woman of about twenty-three was bringing them hot food—surely not at the request of the Master of Broadmoor.

"I am Amanda. I am one of those that Rodann hypnotized and kidnapped. He knows black magic.

I know that because I am a witch. But his power seduced me and he promised me much that he has yet to deliver.

I am his prisoner."

Amanda sat on a bench, careful to leave only a crack of light from the open door—there were ears in this place she said.

"I know you must be hungry and scared—as I was when I arrived.

I took pity on you and since I work in the kitchen I prepared some food—just stew and

warm bread I've just taken from the ovens. It's
not much."

Brianna thanked her and Trevor was eating
voraciously and nodding 'thank you' to Amanda.

"I must tell you two things before I go," Amanda
said.
"First of all—there are other children—girls—
and you must help them. If you manage to get out
of this place—take them! I beg of you!
Second, there is another prisoner. She is the
rightful owner of this castle—Lady Trethewey."

"My mother is *here*?" said Brianna loudly.
Trevor put his hand over her mouth with a
'shush!'

"Yes. Her living quarters are on the upper level
where she has access to the patio and walkways
on the roof. She is never allowed to come down or
go outside.
I didn't know why—until you just spoke—why
she was a prisoner of the Master.
That also explains why he treats her so well—I
mean, for a prisoner.
We prepare fine dishes and take her tea, and
clean her rooms and bath, and wash her clothing
by hand."

She is his insurance," Amanda concluded. "So
long as the owner resides here, her son can claim

he is her caretaker and keeps the property only for her benefit.

I'm not stupid," she said.

"No, you are *not!*" said Brianna, hugging her tight and stroking her face.

"I must go," said Amanda. "God be with you."

The door closed but Trevor did not hear the dreary click of the metal lock.

She had left it open!

"Hold me, Trevor."

Brianna's emotions had run the full gamut today.

Waking in the dungeon, meeting her long-lost brother and confronting him, feeling his spite and seeing his demented mind at work...

And now the astonishing revelation—her mother lived and was so tantalizingly close!

Brianna wanted to run—run up those stairs to the very top of the castle, run into her Mother's arms.

Tears flooded into her eyes and her body shook as Trevor wrapped his arms around her tight and held her, anchoring her, comforting her.

"I've got you! I won't let you go!"

He murmured words of comfort and care and in time the tears subsided and she slept in his embrace, his body warm and strong—her fortress.

Chapter Fourteen   The Dungeon

Brianna was speaking.
"If Mother is senile or infirm then Rodann can claim he is looking after her best interests—including being the resident steward of the property. Amanda is right."

"I think we need to bring this matter to our solicitor," said Trevor. "We want this to go one way, but it seems to want to go another.
The first order of business, however, is getting the hell out of this place!"
"She left the door unlocked for a reason," Brianna reminded him.
"I know. That could be our ticket to escape—or if we get caught, our death sentence. I don't think these fanatics are going to just let us walk out of here," Trevor said.

"Maybe she means for us to find the children," Brianna said.

"And do what?" queried Trevor. "We may put them in grave danger if we so much as speak to them."

"Trevor, we have to *try*! We can't leave them
here to go on being exploited and abused. We just
can't!"

"Alright, then we *won't*. Just give me a second
to think. If we can find a way out, this could work.

I think we need to wait for dark—when
everyone is asleep. We can't take them all—we
will take just *one*. Then we slip out and make our
way to the car, and then make a police report to
the effect that children are being held in captivity
here.
They can't turn their backs on that.

If we have to, we'll go to the news media and
blow this wide open!"

 ***

The problem—they soon realized—is where
were the children kept!
Are there guards to stop them escaping? Are
they chained or locked up?
There were too many loose ends, Trevor
thought.
The hall was quiet. Brianna suggested they
might be in the old servant quarters just off the
kitchens. It would make sense since they were
expected to do the chores of cooking and cleaning.

What little battery life his cellphone still had was enough to light the passageway and Trevor guided them along.

He could hear voices—children's voices. They were near, he thought.

But where exactly? And how can we get to them without raising the alarm? They won't know we're coming for them!

He had an idea, but it was risky.

If he could make it sound like guards were doing inspection or a check on them, he could get them to open the door themselves and then he could explain what he and Brianna had planned.

If there actually *were* guards, he hadn't seen any. He had to take a chance.

Trevor rapped sharply on the servant's room door. He said "Open up!" in a deep male voice.

To his surprise, it was opened quickly by two girls—twins as it turned out.

Brianna tugged on their sleeves to get them out of the room itself and into the corridor so they could explain what was going on.

At first the girls had trouble understanding.

"You have to trust us," said Brianna.
"Just keep quiet and do what we say," said
Trevor.
Do you know if there is an exit to the outside on
this level?" he continued.

"No, not really. They don't permit it," said one
of the girls.

Trevor continued to guide them along this
corridor until they came to a crossing with a
larger passage.
What now? If we get caught now, we're done.

A sudden sound of a door and footsteps
approaching, and Trevor buried his phone in his
pocket—ready to fight for their lives.

One girl sneezed and the footsteps halted.

"Who goes there?" the man's voice challenged.

Trevor flashed his light directly in his eyes,
hoping to disorient him and to punch him hard
enough to remove the threat.
Brianna gasped.
"Terran! It's *me*, the doctor—from the A&E
who treated you...remember?"
She grabbed the phone from Trevor and shone
it in her own face.

"Doctor Hardy? What are you doing *here*?" Terran asked.

"I can't explain right now but we need your help. We need to get out of the castle fast! Can you help?"

Terran signaled to keep voices down and made a gesture to follow him.

Not too far down the wider corridor to the left, he motioned them to an alcove with a door that he unlocked from a set of keys jangling on his belt.

"I have no idea where this takes you—but it will take you to the driveway eventually. You'll have to figure it out," Terran said in a low voice.

"We owe you one, buddy," said Trevor.

"No, you don't. Dr. Hardy saved my life so I'm glad to get a chance to pay it back. Now, hurry!"

The girls were shivering in the damp night air and the lawn was wet with dew and too uneven to walk swiftly.

Soon the gravel began and they crept out of the archway into the main drive, keeping to the side-- although there were no lights to expose them and Trevor thought any cameras would not pick up their tiny troupe as they stealthily crept to the south gate—and freedom.

***

It was very late indeed when Trevor swung the car to the gates of Abbey Grange and spoke briefly to the security person there.

The intercom connected to the Earl's cell and Brianna announced their very unorthodox arrival.

Both the earl and the countess were clad in nightgowns when they entered the front hall.

"My God, you look like you've been in a shipwreck!" said Jodie.
"We'll tell you all about it, but first we need to get these girls some blankets or towels, and afterwards some food and hot tea," said Brianna, hugging Jodie.
"Of course! Jeffrey? Rouse Maria and get her to put out something to eat and put on the kettle.
We'll be down directly," said Jodie.

All the females fled upstairs leaving Trevor kicking off his shoes and tagging after Jeff into the dining room.

The warm floor was a welcome change from the biting cold of the castle and the dungeon.

"Heavens, man! You need something stronger than tea to drink."

Trevor felt the whiskey warming up his insides in a very pleasant way.

By the time the ladies came down, the table had been laid with pastries and cheeses, hot tea and glasses of milk for the twins—Emma and Christine, both eight years of age.

With faces washed and hair combed they looked much prettier and certainly much happier than they were in the smoky darkness of Broadmoor Castle.

"We didn't want to impose but we had no choice," Brianna began. "Thank you for making us welcome. I don't know what we would have done without you."

"We completely understand," said Jodie. "It was just the same twenty years ago when you and your sister landed up on our doorstep."

"And you kept some of our dresses!" marveled Brianna.
Don't these girls look precious in them!"

"Good job we kept the security," said Jeff. "You sure you weren't followed?"

"No other cars on the road," said Trevor.

"Let's have a snack, put the girls to bed and then we can talk about what to do next," said Jodie.

A little later the four adults were seated comfortably on the sofa having a drink.

"Seems to me that we need to be a bit careful," Jeffrey started.
"We don't want to be seen harboring missing children, do we?"

"I think we haven't thought this through," admitted Trevor. "All that was on our mind was escape—and we intended to take only one child; then the twins just appeared."

"Well can we not simply return them? I mean—where do they live? They *do* have parents, don't they?" Jodie was on her second gin & tonic.

"I have no idea," said Brianna. "We just snatched them and ran!"

"See my point?" said Jeffrey. "We can't just be snatching children hither and thither. Word will get out and the police will come round and..."

"Okay, let's do it this way," said Trevor.

"For a few days we let them stay here—if someone inconveniently drops by, we say they are second cousins once removed. That is, distant relatives who happen to be girls—and girls love horses and it's the Christmas break, and so on. Follow me?"

Jodie was getting a little sarcastic as the fears and the gin kicked in.
"Meanwhile, *you* will try to locate their families-- who of course will be grateful to have their children back, so would not *think* of pressing charges for unlawful confinement of minor children? Is that what you mean?"

"I'll go to our solicitor in Shrewsbury first thing in the morning," said Trevor.
"I'll lay out the whole picture for him, and see what he has to say. Worst case—he can provide some legal rationale as to why we should be hailed as heroes who saved two helpless kids."

"Well, we *are*," said Brianna hotly. "We stuck our necks out to do the right thing. Any judge or jury is going to see that right away."

"Alright, " said Jeffrey wearily. "Let's get some rest and pick this up again in the morning."

"Oh, I forgot, Brianna," said Jodie. "The girls are in the upstairs bedroom, and the spare room is being renovated after a ceiling leak.

I will have to put you downstairs in the bedroom adjacent to the study.”

“Fine,” said Brianna. “We’re not fussy.”

“Well, um, there’s just the one queen bed in there. Will that be awkward?”
Jodie didn’t look embarrassed at all. In fact she had a mischievous smile she couldn’t conceal.

Brianna shot a quick glance at Trevor, who pretended not to hear.

“Perfect,” she said evenly. “Does it have a loo?”

The big house was quiet and dark.

Brianna was so tired that she just gave her teeth a quick brushing and slid into the cool sheets.

She thought Trevor was already asleep—and he should have been—but he turned to her in the soft dark and put his hand on her cheek.

“I think you’re pretty special,” he said in a husky voice. “I think I’m going to keep you.”

He slid his hand down to her breast and put his mouth on hers.

That's the last thing Brianna remembered when she woke up, with birds singing outside the windows, and sunlight dancing on the curtains.

***

Alfred David Long--member in good standing of the Bar and an experienced lawyer—was smoking a pipe when Trevor was shown into his inner office.

"Ah, Mr. Gower. You look like you need more sleep! How can I help you today?"

"I have a sticky situation."
Trevor told him everything—including why they were in the castle in the first place.

"And you took some photographs maybe?" said the lawyer.

"Yes, and even a few seconds of video. I don't know why they didn't frisk me and confiscate the camera. Too busy playing 'knights in shining armor' I guess."

"Leave the camera with me, for now. I have an idea that's been cooking in my head and I want to run it by you, Trevor."

Long put his pipe down in an ashtray and took a yellow pad from the drawer of his desk.

He began to sketch the castle—doodling actually—and write down a few words that were unfamiliar to Trevor. Lawyer words.

"What I am thinking is that Rodann, arguably, has a legitimate claim to occupy Broadmoor—especially with the knowledge that Lady Trethewey is—or *may be*—in residence and has tacitly approved of her son and his cronies.

But regardless, I am suggesting that we—'we' meaning Brianna—sue him for Detinue & Conversion, old British legal terms for 'holding and gaining an illicit benefit from property or assets to which you have no legal right, to use or sell for your own benefit.'"

Trevor nursed his cappuccino and continued to listen.

"This would make him a trespasser. This would deprive him of any basis to continue to stay at Broadmoor. Then the Sheriff and his men can go and physically remove him."

"They'd better be good with swords!" said Trevor with a grin. "Hey, how about this?"

We file a Writ of Summons, outlining our whole argument and demand that the Defendant provide a case that disproves our allegations."

Frankly," said the lawyer, "I don't think that's going to happen."

"Why?" Trevor asked.

"First of all, I don't think he has a case to meet ours," said Long.

"Secondly—and this is based on what you have just related to me—I don't think he is normal psychologically anymore; if he *ever* was. So he will be unable to mount a defence in court and we will get judgement in our favor."

"But the police? They are in on this whole sordid affair. They are part of it."

"That's precisely why we don't pursue criminal charges at this juncture; the civil courts will tear Rodann to pieces—if I know anything.

The police have no jurisdiction in civil matters and will be shut out as their bad boy bites the dust!"

The lawyer got so excited that he picked up his pipe, tamped the dottle with his finger, then sucked the flame from his match into the fragrant shreds—releasing a not unpleasant blue cloud of smoke.

Both Trevor's father and grandfather were pipe men so he was used to the smoke and understood why pipes have been smoked for centuries.

Just not his cup of tea though.

"The other thing," said the lawyer out of the corner of his mouth while puffing on the pipe stem, "is this lawsuit will give us leverage in the eyes of the courts when it comes time to face down the authorities.

They have been reluctant to even acknowledge the problem, but once they get wind of the litigation underway, they will start to weaken.

If a judge in Her Majesty's High Court thinks that there is an issue with Broadmoor and its tenants—it will be hard for the police to just shrug and walk away."

A large lazy blue smoke ring drifted over Trevor's head and dissipated near the door.

"I like it!" exulted Trevor. "I think Brianna would approve."

"Let's not forget one thing, Trevor.

In the U.K., just as it is in Canada, it costs money to go to trial. The vast majority of civil suits are settled 'out of court'—that is, an agreement between the opposing parties is reached and their solicitors settle the amount of 'damages' if money is at issue.

In your case, we are seeking a remedy that isn't a quantum of damages but rather is a specific outcome that the plaintiff—Brianna—is seeking."

"So what you are really saying, Mr. Long, is that this thing may be over before it begins."

"Yes, that is what I am saying here, Trevor. I will begin the preparation of the writ and wording of it today. You check back with me Monday next and we'll see what's what at that point in time."

***

"You didn't ask him about what to do with the girls?" Brianna said, clearly annoyed.

"I didn't get to it. I was so excited about the lawsuit, it was all that was in my mind."

Brianna was tired after another brutal shift at the hospital. They ate quickly in town and returned to Abbey Grange.

Trevor had bought Swiss chocolate treats for the girls, flowers for Jodie, and a bottle of single-malt Scotch for Jeff.

Before they got out of the car, he kissed her and said: "I have a plan, sweetie. You're gonna love it!"
Brianna gave him a look that said '*It'd better be good.*'

The girls were thrilled by the candy and rushed up the stairs to their room.

"Ah, Glenmorangie," Jeff said with delight, taking the Scotch to his bar and opening it eagerly.
He poured two glasses and sat down in a wing chair across from the sofa.

"What did your solicitor say?" asked Jodie.

Trevor explained the concepts that the lawyer had presented, and he turned to Jodie.
"What do you think?"

"I think it's brilliant!" she said. "Trust a lawyer to come up with something like this!"

She looked at Jeff impatiently.
"So where's my drink?"

"Sorry, darling."
Jeffrey went to the kitchen to get some ice and a lime and quickly put together a gin and tonic for his wife.
He turned to Brianna.
"What's yours, love?"
"I'll have the same," she said. She preferred a crisp white but these folks were not wine people.
"So...does anybody want to hear my plan?" announced Trevor.
"Yes, of course," said Jodie.

"Here's what we are going to do," he said, putting his whiskey on the coffee table.

"We know now that the twins were abducted in broad daylight from the Market Hall in town nearly five months ago.

The police have let the case go cold, no doubt.

We are going to go at night and deliver the twins right to their own front door, and have them say they escaped from the castle and ran home all the way.
No one will question their story and the parents will be only too happy to have them home.

We can sit them outside for a bit to get cold and wet so they will be believed.
That's it!
Then nobody in *this* house can be subject to prosecution for being an accessory to kidnap."

Brianna snuggled in to Trevor and pulled her knees and feet up on the sofa.

"But I *like* the twins," said Jodie. "Can't we keep them just a little bit longer?"

"For God's sake, Jodie! They're not house pets!" said Jeffrey.
"So it's agreed? We do this tonight!" said Trevor.

"Who's going to coach the girls so they get their story straight?" said Jodie.

"I think you are the perfect choice, Jodie," said Trevor.

"I mustn't feed them, poor things. They have to be famished and frozen when they appear at the door." Jodie and Brianna spoke quietly and both ascended the stairs together.

"One small wrinkle, old chap," said Jeffrey.

"Say!" said Trevor.

"What if there's nobody home?"

"Well, unless the parents have gone to Spain," said Trevor, "I'm going to assume that they will return at some point this evening.

Worst case is that the girls can pound on the neighbors' door. Even if the police are called, if they stick to their guns, they will be saved—and get their names in the paper, and all that."

"With no trail leading back to us," said Jeffrey. "That's very clever of you, Trevor."

"As the old saying goes: 'Necessity is the mother of invention.'"

Chapter Fifteen   The Dragon

Rodann was furious. Four people had escaped his clutches and he took this personally.

"Who was supposed to be watching them?" Rodann was pacing back and forth yelling at anyone and everyone.

"My lord, I was on duty yet heard nothing," said one knight.
"That girl knew the ways of the castle too well," said another.
"Heads will roll if I find out who is responsible!" growled Rodann.

"Meanwhile—find them! Search every nook and cranny of every village from here to Shrewsbury. Then search Shrewsbury! They must be brought to me—alive!"

A door slammed and the bewildered knights spoke among themselves.

"Let's take the work lorries—be sure to dress as utility workers so as to avoid suspicion."

Three vehicles with 'E.ON Energy Solutions' on the side panels were warming up in the lot. Each held three men carrying mobile communication devices—and pistols—and soon sped out the front gates.

A core contingent of guards remained behind.

They organized the remaining children into search parties that began to systematically go through every room in the vast building.

A well-dressed woman and her companion driving a late-model Volvo S60 stopped in Briar Hill outside Wildswallows and just watched, letting the motor run.

Beryl came out to get the post and noticed--but kept her head down until she went back inside.

"They're not from around here, Bill," she said to Bill who was finishing up a late breakfast.

"Got sum'ming to do with this nasty business Brianna has got herself into," he said.

"Lock the front door, love—and put out the NO VACANCY notice in the front window. Don't want them to even set foot here."

Three thirsty electrical workers came storming into the Root & Branch and poked their noses into every corner before settling at the bar.

"Is there some power outage in the village?" the owner asked innocently.

"Nar. Just routine maintenance. Give us a pint will ya," said one bearded fellow. But his eyes roved around the pub constantly as if looking for something or someone.

Niall Watson was looking too, but being very nonchalant in his little corner, hiding behind the newpaper.

The headline glared: FUGITIVES ON THE LOOSE and gave details from the police about two adults and two children who were wanted by the police and who needed the public's help in apprehending them.

The men paid up and left in a hurry.

The owner shot a look at old Niall, who nodded and winked back at him. Niall understood everything--as the locals well knew.

Bayston Hill was next--with the same scenario.

Three scruffy utilities men tramp into the local pub, peering around and poking their face into the Men's, before settling for a quick pint—followed by a quick exit.

"Has this to do with the fugitives?" asked the owner to whoever was at the bar.

"Dunno," came the universal reply.

"Why haven't they got uniformed constables then? If this is a police matter, they should have regular cops. Just a coincidence, I guess."

"Aye," everyone replied.

And so it went--in all the likely areas for the fugitives to have fled to.

In one popular watering hole in Shrewsbury, the utility personnel went so far as to issue a threat to anyone withholding information.
That caused a stir.

But not as much as the newspaper story of the late edition of the *Chronicle.*

Apparently a local lawyer had released details of a supposed kidnapping ring that had nabbed local children in the county and was holding them at Broadmoor Castle—already the subject of an urban legend concerning spooky stuff up there.

Brianna and Trevor would only find this out the next day when Jeff came in from shopping with the newspaper in his hand.

"Where did they get this picture of the twins?" he said accusingly to Trevor.

Trevor grabbed the paper and showed Brianna.

"I didn't give it to him," Trevor told Jeff.

"Then *explain* how *your* lawyer got hold of this photograph?"

Trevor studied it. *Did I take this photo...? I don't remember doing it.*

Then he noticed the background was the door of the townhouse—complete with number—that they had dropped off Emma and Christine the other night, having followed Trevor's bold plan.

"This was taken by someone else. See? That's their front door; so it must be the parents who took this and reported the incident to police."

"How did our solicitor get in, then?" Brianna asked.

"I'm going to go out on a limb here," Trevor said, "but I think Alfred David Long has an inside contact in the Shrewsbury Police.
Unless he happened to be at the station and someone happened to leave the photo lying on the counter and he happened to put it in his briefcase on his way out."

"Really?" said Jodie.

"Think about it," said Trevor.

"This is a political disaster for the cops. They are doing their level best to keep the whole scandalous thing at Broadmoor a secret.

If someone gets wind of it, they are in deep trouble. And that means Rodann is now an endangered species!

I'm not going to ask Long 'how' and 'who'—I'm just going to watch the public's reaction to this story."

Trevor--and the entire Shrewsbury community—did not have to wait very long.

   ***

Parents and school officials, nurses and social workers—all were demanding an answer. All had experienced the sudden and random disappearance of children as young as eight over the last couple of years or so.

All had duly reported the missing children to police and all had been given the same bland response: *We are looking into the matter and assure you that all that can be done IS being done.*
The End.

Most had given up—including the police who let these cases go cold for lack of evidence, they said.

But now it was big news. The media jumped on it.

"Should we...go to the police?" said Brianna. "I mean, we really ought to."

"Not a good idea," said Jeff.

"Let's let the snowball roll a bit more down the hill," said Trevor.
"Once these parents and public health people get their teeth into this, they won't let go until they have the answers they have wanted--and deserved--all this time."

"Do the police have to disclose what they know?" asked Jodie.

"I don't think they have a choice," said Trevor. "This story will ripple to the bigger centers like Birmingham and London. Police and government officials are going to be all over this.

There will surely be an investigation.

Before that day comes, the Chief and the Vice-Chief will be dancing on one foot to show that they have exercised proper methods and sent a team to the castle to find out what truth there may be in the story."

"And the television reporters will be right along with them," said Jeff. "This is going to put Shrewsbury law enforcement under a microscope."

"Exactly right," said Trevor.

"Do you think they will come for us?" said Brianna nervously.

"I don't see why," said Trevor. "All they know is that there may be children in forced and unlawful confinement at the castle and they will need a search warrant to determine if that is the case.

Nobody but the twins—and of course Rodann—even know that we are involved. And for the moment--until it's time to make our move—I want to keep it that way."

   ***

"Trevor, I'm sorry. I've got you into all this."

They were having breakfast with Jodie and Jeff and apprehensive about what news the day would bring.

"I *chose* this, Brianna. I promised I would stand beside you through it all. And I will."

"You don't get an offer like that every day," said Jodie, pouring tea.

"I'm afraid you'll waste your whole sabbatical fighting dragons—for my sake," Brianna said.

Only later—when the meal was over and Trevor pulled her into the bedroom—would she hear what she had dreamed of hearing.

"After this is over, I am staying on sabbatical, I'm not going back to Toronto.
I decided that a couple of weeks ago and now that everything has come to a head—I'm certain about this."
Trevor seized her impulsively and pulled her to his body.
"Brianna. I love you. I could not think of being apart from you. Don't send me away!"

Their kiss was deeper than the night sky full of stars.

A sudden knock at the door brought them back from the heaven they had found.

"Sorry. Did I interrupt something?" said Jodie.

"Have a look at today's headlines! She crowed thrusting the daily paper in their faces.

POLICE MAKE SHOCKING DISCOVERY AT CASTLE
The subheading added: *Heroic actions of local police save children from evil cult.*

Brianna smoothed her hair and took Trevor's arm as they alighted on the sofa.

There was a glow on their faces that Jodie noticed but declined to comment on.

"They brought in special constables and called for SO19—a tactical response unit with serious firepower," said Jeff.
"We don't normally have coppers packing .45s or guns of any kind—unlike you in Canada and the U.S.
But we have paramilitary personnel who do."

Jeff had poured a Scotch and was eagerly sucking it back.

"I wonder who gave the order?" Jeff continued. "My understanding is that only someone close to the Prime Minister can give the order for this kind of operation."

Brianna was not really listening. Her head rested on Trevor's shoulders and her eyes were closed.

"Let's see what's on the telly tonight," said Jodie.
"Yes," agreed Jeff. "I want to see this *live*," he said, draining his glass.
The room was darkened for effect as Jodie switched on the television; dramatic music played

as the live broadcast took the audience to County Shropshire—to Broadmoor Castle.

Good evening, this is the BBC. We are coming to you live from the lovely Shropshire Hills south of Shrewsbury to bring you this special news report.

Trevor and Jeff clinked bottles of local brew and smiled broadly.

Shrewsbury Police have done some fine legwork to uncover a kidnapping ring led by an apparently deranged leader who calls himself 'Rodann'.

We will go into the backstory of this strange cult later in our programme...

The camera shone in the faces of at least a dozen children wrapped in blankets as they were ushered into waiting police vans.

ITV, BBC, the *Shropshire Star* and of course--the *Chronicle*--all had boots on the ground with a forest of microphones and spotlights--turning the night into day in a place that had been shrouded in shadow for so long.

Burly officers led several men—some dressed like knights in period costume—to waiting cars as camera flashes added to the surreal scene.

The BBC team got in for a close-up with the Chief.

When did you first realize there was criminal activity here at the castle, Chief?

"Well, we received confidential information from an insider that confirmed our own suspicions. We had this whole thing under surveillance for some time and waited to make our move."

How does it feel to know that parents are grateful to you and the force for saving their little ones?

"I can only say that Shrewsbury's finest are superb at what they do and we are indeed pleased to crack this ring of child slavery at last!"

"I'm going to puke," said Trevor. "This douchebag was at the center of this thing the whole time!"

"*Douchebag?*" said Jodie dubiously.

"One of many Canadian idioms we have for despicable people," said Trevor.

"Oh, I see. Lovely to learn a new word from time to time," she said.

Now the ringleader is being brought out, said the newsman.

The camera panned to a miserable looking Rodann in handcuffs, glowering at the crowd, before being stuffed into the back of a cruiser.

Police inform us that charges will be laid for kidnapping, forcible confinement, confinement of minors using duress, and child abuse and neglect.

There may be others, the Chief said, but they will wait for the Crown Prosecutors to make that decision.

This is Harjinder Singh reporting from the Shropshire Hills near Briar Hill.

"Good job!" shouted Jeffery.

"This would not have been possible had it not been for your bravery--Brianna and Trevor," said Jodie.

"I still can't believe this is real," said Brianna.

"At some point we will surface," said Trevor, "probably through the civil action we started.

We still don't have the keys to the front door, and we still don't know who will take care of Lady Trethewey.

Lots of loose ends."

"I'm so happy for those children!" Jodie said.

"Yes, you are right. That is the best thing of all!" said Brianna.

"I suppose we'll never hear from the twins again," said Jodie dolefully.

"We might—you never know," said Brianna.

Chapter Sixteen   Twists and Turns

The investigation was going to take some time, Brianna learned.

The castle and its grounds were off-limits to everyone except law enforcement personnel.

A special forensic team was sent from London CID to collect DNA and fingerprints on all kinds of items of interest.

This included ceremonial hardware including alleged torture devices in the basement and sub-basement areas.

Carpeting, towels—any clothing was targeted.

Doors and windows, railings and bannisters—latex gloves, facemasks and swabs were the new costumes worn at Broadmoor Castle.

Trevor applied for—and was denied—a special pass to gain access to the building.

"But my mother is a prisoner there!" exclaimed Brianna at the gate.

"No one is a prisoner anymore, madam," said the tall sergeant.

"Have you checked? Where is the old lady in white who lives at the top floor? What have you done with her?"

"I can assure you, madam...". He was cut off by a female superintendent who intervened.

"The old lady who was in residence upstairs has been transferred to a facility in Birmingham for elderly patients," she explained.

"Patient? Why is she a patient?" demanded Brianna. "I'm a doctor, for God's sake. I have to see her!"

"She received an initial assessment by one of our medical people after she had been evacuated.
     Their opinion is that she is suffering from advanced senility—and possibly dementia brought on by her privation in the castle."

"She is my mother! Tell me where she is being kept. I must go to her."

"Show me some identification, Miss, and I will be happy to provide the information you seek," said the supervisor.

"It would have been nice if someone had told you," said Jodie.

"How could they, pet?" said Jeff soothingly.
     "Nobody knew Brianna was in the picture so nobody at the castle was going to be of help.
     It's a good job you went up today, Brianna," Jeff said. "Now you know what they have done with her and can visit on your day off."

"Let's turn on the evening news," said Trevor. "Might be able to glean some useful information."

Police tonight have locked down Broadmoor Castle as their investigators comb through its vast interior looking for evidence to support the charges laid earlier this week against Robert 'Rodann' Hardy and his co-conspirators.

DNA has been collected and photographs seized which show bizarre rituals and bacchanalian orgies were performed on the premises.

Brianna looked right at Trevor. He shrugged.

Investigators from as far away as Scotland Yard in London have heaped praise on the local police in Shrewsbury and their intrepid Chief for cracking this horrible case.
More details as they become available.

"Indeed!" said Jeffrey.

"If you'd like, I will drive you to Birmingham," said Jodie. "I need a day away and there's a lovely dress shop I know."

"I'd love that," responded Brianna. "How about Friday morning? I think I might get Gemma to cover for me for the afternoon."

***

There was a fairly new senior residence that was part of the University Teaching facilities for Med students and social workers. Brianna had not seen it as it was outside of her specialty—acute trauma and injury.

The front desk nurse took them up.
"Your daughter is here, Mrs. Hardy," said the nurse in an exaggerated tone.
"She's lost some of her hearing," the nurse said, pulling back the white curtains around the bed.

Estelle Hardy was hooked up to an IV unit dispensing glucose, and had the side rails elevated to prevent a fall or other mishap.

"Mummy? Mummy can you recognize me? It's your daughter--Brianna!"

The old woman roused and asked for the bed to be cranked up so she could face her visitors.

At 81, Estelle Hardy was hardly in any shape to be wandering around an old damp castle the nurse said.
"Brianna? Is that you?" said Estelle.

Brianna lowered the left side rail and threw herself on her mother's breast. She could not control the tears that came out like a gust of wind.

"Lady Trethewey? Do you know me?

I am Jeffrey Hardy's wife—Jodie," said Jodie, joining Brianna at the bedside.

"We've brought you some lovely flowers!"

The nurse helped arrange them in the vase and then said she had to go look in on another patient.

"Jeffrey? Earl of Trent? You must be the Countess," said Estelle—now awake and aware of what was going on.

"Switch on the light and let me have a look at you," the old lady said.

"How did you find me?"

"Brianna found you. Brianna has been staying with us," Jodie said. She did not mention Trevor.

"We have been so worried—you cooped up in the castle like that. They've closed it up for now— the police."

"The police?" said Estelle in a bewildered tone of voice. "Whatever do the police want?"

"Mum. They've arrested Rodann. He's been up to some very bad things at Broadmoor and there is an investigation on," said Brianna.

"Oh they've been a noisy bunch those ragamuffins. But I've grown used to it. There's a lovely girl named...ah..."

"Amanda?" offered Brianna.

"Oh yes—Amanda. She's been with me. She helps me manage. Such a nice girl!" said Estelle.

Jodie gave Brianna a quizzical look.
"I'll tell you later," she whispered and Jodie nodded.

"When can I go back?" Estelle was saying.

"Dunno, Mum. We've got to get you sorted first," said Brianna.

"I wanted to put some daffodil bulbs in this Fall but I haven't got round to it," said Estelle.

"For the time being we are going to keep you here, Mum. They will take good care of you."

"Oh I don't mind. I'm much warmer here than at the estate. All my joints have stiffened up and I know jolly well that is because of that old damp place.
You must help me get the heaters working again. We've got lots to do, dear. Your father would help if only he were here."

Brianna sat very still and looked at her mother.

"What do you know of Dad? Where is he?"

Her voice was full of emotion as the deep wound began to throb in her chest.

"Why he passed away, dear.
 Before Rodann brought me home—during the time we were moving about.
 During the time we..." and now Estelle began to sob in great choking breaths and her eyes flooded with tears.

"They took you away from us!" Estelle began to shout. "They took you and would not tell us!"

"Who took them, Lady Trethewey?" said Jodie now holding the old lady's frail hand in hers.

"Men. I don't know. These men took my husband and me to a small town and put us up in a flat. They said it was not safe to be at the castle. They said we could be hurt.
 But they never said where they took you girls! Brianna! My beautiful daughter! Where is your sister? Where have they taken her?"

The old woman began to rave--bringing staff in to check on her.
 "Blood pressure very high," said the nurse removing the cuff.
 "I'm a physician," said Brianna showing her badge. "I give you permission to administer a sedative at this time."

"Right, I'll go to the dispensary," the nurse said and she slipped into the hall.

Brianna touched her mother's shoulder and gently rubbed her back in a circular motion.

"Mum. Beryl's fine. Beryl's living in Briar Hill. She's gone and married a nice chap, Mum. I'll bring her round next time I come, okay?"

The nurse brought the medication and let Brianna give it to her mother with a glass of water.

Then she lowered the bed frame with the crank so Estelle could sleep.

Jodie knew Brianna was burning to hear the truth from her mother's lips, but Brianna raised the rail in place until it clicked securely.

Brianna lowered herself close to her mother and gently kissed her forehead.

"Rest, Mummy, rest until I return. I love you so much." She choked back tears.

"Yes, dear. Love. Dear...love," murmured Estelle Hardy.
And she was out.

Jodie and Brianna thanked the attending nurse and Brianna slipped her a business card with a number where she could be reached.

"Come. I've famished," said Jodie. "There's a decent café just over one or two streets—I forget.
Let's grab a bite before we get on the motorway. I'll text Jeffrey and let them know when we can be expected home."

****

"Well is she *all there*? Or not?" Jeff started the conversation after dinner.

"Oh, Jeffrey! Why is that relevant?" said Jodie.

"Well it may be the deciding factor in the eyes of the court as to who gets possession of the castle," he replied.

"What is going on with your solicitor, Trevor?" said Jodie.

"He has filed a brief with the civil court in which he establishes a *prima facie* case against Rohann for detinue & conversion, that is, for unlawfully denying the family use of the castle as a residence and using it for his own profit and benefit."

"What good will that do? He's in jail!" replied Jodie.

"What it does is permanently exclude Rohann from ever setting foot in the place again.
Remember, we started the lawsuit as a way to get around police obstruction in our efforts to get at Rohann. Nobody could have guessed that things would take a turn as they have.

So, regardless of what the criminal court decides, he is out!"
Trevor paused.
"And therefore, I have instructed our solicitor to bring a motion in court to appoint Brianna as the legitimate tenant, and as joint custodian of the estate along with her sister Beryl."

"Jolly good!" said Jeff. "That's super!"

"You have a good legal head on your shoulders," said Jodie. "Pity you didn't become a lawyer instead of a stuffy historian and scholar.
Sorry. I tend to call 'em like I see 'em," she said.

"I gave it some thought," said Trevor. "But there are too many fascinating and unanswered questions in archaeology and history to ignore!"

But Jodie wasn't done.

"So you'll be going back to your Canada I suppose? You have a good position in a college there, I've heard."

Brianna was looking at him too. *Had he changed his mind? Was his promise the other night just a fleeting impulse?*

"I suppose it's time for me to lay my cards on the table," Trevor said.
"Ever since I came to England to give a talk at Cambridge I couldn't get it out of my mind.
Before I left for London the first time, I started having dreams about a ghost, and a young woman. My first night in Britain I had the same dream!
I was confused about what they might mean.

I thought it was maybe related to the strange artifact that I was carrying or the crazy quest I was on.
Or perhaps the dream was a message from the Beyond. Perhaps I was being guided to come here.

When I saw Brianna I recognized her as the girl with the golden hair in my dream. I felt as if I knew her on some deep level, like she was my soulmate.
I never told you, Brianna, about any of this."

Trevor went on.

"I knew I had to see her again—if nothing else clear up my own doubts and put my hypothesis to the test.

When she sent me the message that brought me to Briar Hill I was beginning to think I was losing my mind.

Officially, I came to the UK to do research for a series of papers I want to write.

I know that amazing primary resources exist at England's universities—stuff I just cannot get to--unless I come in person."

Trevor took the beer Jeff offered and then continued.

"But since I have been here I have come to know Brianna and how wonderful she is. I wasn't expecting anything to happen between us."

He paused and then took Brianna's hand.

Jodie gasped as Trevor slid off the couch on one knee to face Brianna.

"Brianna? Will you marry me? I promise to love you always and forever."

And all present gasped when he took a small box from his jacket pocket and--opening it—revealed a sparkling diamond ring that radiated light to every corner of the room.

Brianna had no chance to prepare for this.

"Trevor…I…yes…yes—I will marry you."
Trevor sat beside her as they embraced in that
perfect moment when the stars align and the
angels sing.

"Put it on!" Jodie's voice was breaking with
happiness. "Where's the ring?"

Trevor slid the band of gold holding its
magnificent gem onto Brianna's left ring finger.

"It's…too beautiful for words," said Brianna.

Trevor mumbled it was a diamond from the Far
North of Canada.

"You bought this *before* you came back to
England?" said Jodie incredulously.

"I don't know why," Trevor said.

"Maybe it was the dream that awakened
something in me that had been sleeping.
I knew it was silly to buy an engagement ring
for somebody I didn't even *know*."
He looked at her adoringly.
"I didn't know if Brianna had a man in her life."

"Well—she does now!" said Jeff enthusiastically pumping Trevor's hand. "Congratulations!"

Brianna couldn't stop tearing up—which made Jodie's eyes moist as well. They were hugging each other like two schoolgirls.

"I think I will have to have a word with Father McMahon at St. Mary's," Jeff was saying to nobody in particular.
Anyway, no one was listening.

As if on cue, the distant sound of church bells could be heard ringing over the fields and valley of the River Severn.
It was Sunday. A day of blessings for new beginnings.

Chapter Seventeen   Farewell, Camelot

After a preliminary hearing in Magistrate's Court, the criminal trial of Robert 'Rohann' Hardy was moved to the Crown Court in Birmingham.

The charges were serious and the prosecution recommended a High Court judge preside.
The Defence had waived its election to trial-by-jury.
The Defence counsel was unlikely to find a sympathetic jury anywhere in the country.

The courtroom was full, of course.
Everyone remotely related to the scandal was fighting to get a seat. A video link was set up in two alternate rooms to accommodate the public and media.

A parade of witnesses were seated behind the bar—the little fence that separates the real players from the audience.

The judge entered to "All rise!" and the indictments were read aloud by the clerk.

They were serious crimes with dire consequences, but the Crown had one more to add

to the list that was entirely unexpected—and
carried a death sentence.

*And in the opinion of Her Majesty's Queen's
Counsel, the accused has been further charged with
treason and conspiracy to foment rebellion against
Her Majesty's government.*

Treason traditionally was the most serious
accusation that could be made against an
individual in the United Kingdom of Great Britain.
The legal team of barristers and solicitors
assigned to defend Rohann would have their work
cut out for them.

Entering a plea of 'not guilty' to all charges,
Rohann took his seat in the prisoner's box.

He had cleaned up considerably and--with
short haircut and natty worsted suit--he looked
like a stockbroker more than a terrorist.

The struggle between Defence and Prosecution
was fierce. As each charge is tabled—each side
argues why the charge is—or is not--justified in
light of the evidence.
All the Defence has to prove is that there is
'reasonable doubt' that he, personally, committed
the offence.
And to do that, two fundamental issues in
criminal law have to be addressed.

First, did he have the *mens rea*—the intent to do something criminal?

Second, did he actually physically do something—anything—to expedite that criminal act?

For example, did he load the gun? tie the knot? order the kidnapping?

In other words, *take action*—because intent to break the law without some specific wrongful action is not sufficient.

A man might truly *want* to rob the bank—but unless he enters the bank and sticks a gun in the face of the teller while demanding money, he is just a guy with a nasty fantasy in the eyes of the law.

In other words, there would be 'reasonable doubt' that the robber could have robbed the bank. He might have been packing a pistol for other reasons, his lawyer could argue. Say...self-defence.

According to the principles of British justice, an accused criminal is entitled to a fair and open trial wherein he or she can offer a defence and challenge the Crown's position.

This is democracy. This is to prevent an innocent person from going to prison for a crime they did not—or could not be proven to—commit.

Trials could last for some days—sometimes weeks. No one could predict this one.

All day long, each charge was tabled and argued--with witnesses and forensic evidence presented by the Crown—and duly attacked or rebutted by the Defence barrister.

Particularly poignant were the testimonies of the children--being of sufficient age to appreciate the nature of the proceedings and the importance to tell the truth of what they experienced and saw.

There were moments of genuine horror as they spoke of physical and sexual abuse.

One girl of about twelve extended her arms for the court to see: there were scars and livid red gashes barely healed where bloodletting had been performed.

When asked who did these heinous things, she pointed an accusing finger at the man in the prisoner's box—Rodann!

The audience collectively inhaled sharply with outrage and shock.

When the court clerk invited the witness to step down, there was vigorous applause— although this was not permitted by the rules of court.

Then it was Amanda's turn.

Dressed modestly, without any jewellery, and with very little makeup--she spoke in a clear voice and told the court how and why she came to Broadmoor.

She described how Rodann seduced her and then trapped her into serving the Order.

The judge and the audience seemed sympathetic when she said--that despite being a sex slave of sorts—she made a commitment to the Lady Trethewey to attend to her needs and care, and that this is how she survived psychologically over the months of exploitation and misery.

The Court announced a recess until 'tomorrow morning at nine a.m.' and the gallery slowly emptied into a hall full of chatter and discussion.

Trevor and Brianna had not attended, so they were eager to see the evening news on television. They were not disappointed.

The reporter showed video clips of the witnesses giving plaintive testimony with regard to not only Rodann's behaviour and treatment, but the whole experience of dungeons and servitude under conditions that—as the Prosecutor had said--'had not been seen in Great Britain since the Dark Ages'.

Not coincidentally, the Shrewbury Chief of Police was on hand to give his two cents worth on local television.

Jeff was yelling at the screen.

"Bollocks! Liar!" and so on. Trevor was in full support and even the ladies were hurling insults at the fraudster on camera.

There would be no trial for all those local influential people who participated in the outrageous 'ceremonies' which had inevitably involved children in captivity.
Local councilmen, bank managers, business owners and their wives—there were many hands that were dirty in Shrewbury and West Midlands.

It was *their* money and *their* silence that had allowed it to continue.

But it was a losing proposition to invite the police to lay charges against these people.
In any case, the local prosecutor and magistrate would have been loathe to proceed, if charges *had* been laid. Too much at stake.

"Switch the channel, Jeffrey," said Jodie. "I think we've seen enough."

"Oh, by the way," said Trevor. "A local chapter of the Arthurian Circle has requested to look at and purchase some of the artifacts collected by the knights at Broadmoor."

Jeff started laughing.
"What? A bloody garage sale is it?"

They all laughed at his inference: garage sale at a medieval castle!

"Well, the stuff might go to a good home, as it were, and we will be rid of it," said Trevor.

"But I thought the place was shut due to the investigation?" said Jodie.

"I've got confirmation by e-mail from the Superintendent that the investigation has concluded and that I will be allowed unrestricted access to the castle," Brianna announced.

"Hurrah!" said Jeff. As always, when it was after dinner and he was in a good mood, he reached for the Scotch on the sideboard.

"And when will this all take place?" asked Jodie.

"Can you help us arrange it? I've got Beryl and Bill to help as well, and I have a rare day off at the week-end," said Brianna.

"Cheers!" said Jeff and Jodie nodded her approval.

"Oh. And bring some gloves and old clothes. It will be dusty and dirty work," said Brianna.

She curled up beside Trevor on the couch—he kissed her and lay an afghan throw across her lap.

But tomorrow would bring another e-mail from the County Clerk that would seem to throw a wrench in their plans—or as the English say: 'A spanner in the works.'

***

Brianna read it twice, poured another cup of tea, and read it again.

According to some archaic regulation that English law is often tangled up with, Brianna can only claim her right to occupy Broadmoor under the common law rules of succession.

The clerk said that unless and until her father's will is found and probated by the court, she only has a temporary right of residence—not an absolute and permanent one.

The letter went further.

If she chooses to cohabit with another person in which sexual intimacy occurs—or can be expected to—that person must be recognized by the courts as a 'spouse'.

In effect, the county will not grant a permit of occupancy to Trevor since his relationship with the lawful applicant is 'undetermined'.

"I just want to laugh," said Brianna.

"Who makes up these regulations?" said Jodie. "Are they from the Victorian Era?"

"It's none of their bloody business!" retorted Brianna. "None at all!"

"So what are you going to do?" said Jodie. "You could write back and say 'There will be NO sex'."

"Oh great! I just get engaged to be married but cannot be intimate with my fiancé. Why are these things happening to *me*? Haven't I suffered enough?"

Brianna was steamed and Jodie was feeling the frustration too.

"I'm calling our solicitor Mr. Long. He must have a solution. He's damned smart and has helped us enormously so far."

"Yes, darling," said Jodie. "Billing at £200 per hour, I am sure he will come up with something!"

"I have to get to work, Jo. Can you drive me? Trevor's in Birmingham with some old fuddy-duddy professor discussing his artifacts."

"Sure. Let me throw on some jeans and a top. Be just two secs."

***

Both Brianna and Trevor came home late.
Brianna was dog-tired and wanted to eat a little—then hit the hay.
Trevor wanted to eat and talk about what he had done in the city.

Since both Jodie and Jeff had already retired for the evening, Brianna prevailed.

"You won't believe what I've discovered, Brianna," he said, covering her face with kisses as she pulled up the sheet and turned out the bedside lamp.

"Wonderful, darling, we can talk about it in the morning, okay?"

"OK, sweetheart. I can't sleep so I'm going to go down for a nightcap. I promise not to wake you when I come up."

"Night, my lovely historian." She reached up to meet his lips and then flopped back and turned on her side.

Trevor lay out the parchment on the rosewood table in the study.

It was not very large: maybe 24 inches long by 18 inches wide.

But since he had located its hiding place in the library in his home, he had not let it out of his sight.

This was precious—if for no other reason than his Grandfather had carefully inscribed it with a nib pen and india ink, then hidden it from everyone.

Did he believe that Trevor might be the one to find it?

What if *nobody* had found it? Would all that effort and research be lost?

Trevor considered that possibility.

So, why *had* Grandfather hidden it in the first place?

The only thing that came to mind was that someone else wanted the secret as well— someone who wanted to get their hands on that information—and might kill to get it!

That *had* to be why it was encrypted using the simple Caesar Code—which was useful to hide the information but easy to decode in the right hands.

J. Rossili Gower would return to Britain soon after—and would mysteriously die suddenly.

It all seemed like Howard Carter's fate after he disturbed the Tomb of Tutankhamun—sudden death, allegedly because of a 'curse' that would fall on anyone who touched the sacred tombs of the Pharoahs.

Was there a curse on this discovery? Would it cost Trevor his life to reveal the secret?

He tried to shake this dark thought out of his head. *Anyhow, I'm still alive, aren't I? I have translated the coded message and I have the secret in my hand!*

The door to the study swung open and Trevor jumped about two feet.

"Holy crap, Jeff! You scared the shit outta me!"
"Sorry, Trev—I heard someone pacing in here and just wanted to have a peek. Just wanted to make sure nobody had broken in—we had some troubles with that years ago, remember?"

"Pour us a drink, Jeff. I've made an exciting discovery. I want to bounce some theories off your head."

Both men were sitting down, legs outstretched as the alcohol started to work.

"Do you remember Howard Carter and the curse of Tutankhamun?" said Trevor.

"'Course! Scared me to death when I was a kid! Plus we watched all those mummy movies! Remember 'Curse of the Mummy'?"
Jeff was warming up to the topic.

"Oh God, yes! Why do those movies always have some helpless woman--with nice tits in a tight blouse--who's going to get grabbed by some guy who's been dead for three thousand years?" Trevor said.

"Haha, that's so boys like us will pay to see the movie again!" said Jeff.

"Well, do you think curses were real? I mean that's my point about Carter. I'm sure there have been others.
In fact, the guy who bankrolled Carter--George Herbert, 5th Earl of Carnarvon--died suddenly four months later from an alleged mosquito bite.
Note that he was present at the tomb when it was opened!" continued Trevor.
"The story is that eleven people in total all died violently in the first ten months of that tomb being opened," Trevor said.

"Geez, you're giving me goosebumps, mate. I need another whiskey," said Jeff.

"Sir Archibald Douglas-Reid—the man who x-rayed the mummy of the dead pharaoh died two years later from a mysterious illness.

Other victims of the curse were shot or jumped to their deaths from windows.

Oh yes my dear Jeffrey, it was a bad business, a bad business."

"Maybe we should get you your own radio show, Trevor? You tell creepy stories very well!"

Both men laughed.

"But seriously, my grandfather died suddenly and mysteriously not long after he visited me and my parents in Toronto about 25 years ago.

He left something unusual in a hidden closet just before he returned to Bristol.

The two items he left I have brought with me and carried in my backpack for months."

Jeff feigned horror and pretended to be choked by an invisible hand.

"The curse! The curse!" he said.

"Okay. Make fun of me if you will. But I still would very much like to know what happened to cause his death.

He seemed fine to me.

Although I do recall he seemed feverish and excited about something. But for whatever reason, he kept it to himself.

And then we got word of his demise."

Jeffrey looked at him.

"So are you thinking you want to see the death
certificate or hospital records?
What year was it?
Yes, I remember the influenza was bad that
year in the UK. Carried off quite a number of
elderly and young infants. They are the
vulnerable ones, you know."
Jeff looked down.
"I lost my Gran that year from flu," he said.

"I'm sorry," said Trevor.
"Not *your* fault. It happens," said Jeff.
"At any rate, it's late. Luckily we both have
gorgeous women with warm bodies to cuddle up
with on this February night. Shall we?"

Trevor left the parchment open on the table as
he left—turning out the light.

***

A late winter storm brought an accumulation of
snow and ice to the West Midlands.

Brianna was sent home early as the hospital
was largely empty of new emergency patients.

Jodie had cooked steaks and everyone
appreciated how tasty supper was that night.

After dinner, they retired to the living room for a drink and to cozy up near the fireplace.

Trevor whispered something in Jeff's ear; Jeff whispered back: "Right. No mention of 'curse'."

"What are you boys whispering about?" asked Jodie—ever the sharp-eyed one.

"Well, Trevor has something he wants to share with us. It's in the study. Shall we move in there?" said Jeff.

"I want to stay by the fire," said Brianna.

"We'll come back," said Trevor putting an arm around his lady and tugging her affectionately.

"Oh. That old thing," Brianna said when she saw what was on the table.

"What is it?" Jodie asked.

"A message left for me by my late grandfather," said Trevor.
"And it's so important that you carried it all the way to Shrewsbury England?" said Jodie.

"It's one of the reasons why I came," said Trevor. "I needed some help with translation. It's in code."

Trevor looked puzzled.

"Jeff? Come over here. Look at this."

"What is it?" Jeff said.

"The script, the writing. It's starting to fade out! Does the sun shine in this window?" Trevor asked. "Like—does it fall on this spot, on the table?"

"I suppose," answered Jodie. "We like to get some sun in here for the plants."

"But your notations are in pencil," said Jeff. "They have not faded one iota."

"What does it say?" asked Brianna finally. "I know this has been on your mind for ages, darling. You used to virtually sleep with this scroll when we were at Wildswallows."
She touched his shoulder and gave him a tender look.

"I have finally decoded it all," he said.

L KDYH IRXQGWKH WKH VHFFUHW.

Everyone stared at the nonsensical words.

L KDYH VROYHG WKH PBVWUB

"Okay, translation," said Jeff.

"It says: 'I have found the secret. I have solved the mystery.'" Trevor said. "That's how the message begins."

"What does the rest of the message say?" asked Brianna.

"It says: 'The Holy Grail is not a cup at all. It is the mystical center within our Consciousness and its physical site is The Third Eye.
Open that and know--at last--the truth of Jesus' words 'The Kingdom of Heaven is within you'.'"

"The Holy Grail!" exclaimed Jeff. "The whole world has been searching for the Holy Grail for twenty centuries!
Are we saying here that your ancestor discovered what no man could?"

"I really don't know, Jeff.
"What I do know is that J. Rossili spent entire years of his retirement researching the Grail, reading the legends—including the King Arthur Grail Quest legend—and I have to assume that this was his *conclusion*."

"So are you going to tell anybody?" Jodie said.

"I intend to publish a series of papers that outline Grandfather's mission and goal—and then, as he would have wanted I think—share the message with the world," Trevor said.

"I *don't* think he wanted this to be kept secret forever. But neither did he want to just come out with it.

I think he wanted me to work on it and once I had decided it was authentic and important—I would be the one to tell.

That's what I feel," Trevor said.

"Oh darling, I am so proud of you," said Brianna throwing herself into his arms.

"This is really something!" said Jeff.

"You do us proud indeed!" said Jodie.
Now can we get out of this freezing room and back to the fireside?"

Chapter Eighteen   The King Is Dead

Friday is usually the busiest day in the Accidents & Emergency Dept. of any hospital in Britain.

Much of that is related no doubt to the fact that on weekends people let loose of all their tension and stress—especially with a pint or three.

Car accidents, fights and quarrels, crossing the street without looking—there are dozens of ways to get hurt.

Brianna was usually on duty or on call on Fridays—meaning she got to see Shrewsbury's underside, and not just the injured.

Addicts who overdose, prostitutes who get assaulted, homeless people pulled in from the bitter cold ten minutes before their heart stops beating.

She'd seen it all.

The hardest ones were the suicides. Suicide is so tragic and leaves heartbreak wherever it happens—including the ambulance and police services who find the victim, these selfless people who suffer vicarious trauma and yet suffer in silence.

Trevor knew all this and took special care to make sure Brianna had time to decompress from the fatigue and emotional impact of being an emergency room doctor.

This Friday had been emotionally draining in another way for her.

This was the day her half-brother Rodann was sentenced by the Crown Court to be sent to prison for a lengthy stretch of time.

She knew he had been evil, she knew he was probably right out of his mind, but she loved him in her own way.

Both Brianna and Trevor were there in the gallery to bear witness to the tragic life and pathetic dreams of someone who was her family.

The court clerk asked the prisoner if he would like to make a final statement before the court prior to being sentenced.

Rodann stood alone—his feet shackled and his hands at his side.

"You do realize, sir," began the Crown attorney, "that what you have perpetrated is not only criminal, but also morally and spiritually misguided and has caused great harm to many?"

Rodann shifted his weight and then spoke.

"Great men—like King Arthur—are seldom recognized in their own time for their victories and glory.

It is their fate to be punished for the sins of others, and to be pilloried on the altar of public opinion, paying the debt of society with their own lives.

If I have done wrong, it is that I spoke up for England, for the Celtic Race--whose blood runs in our veins and has watered the soil of our land again and again in heroic sacrifice.

Remember not what *I* have done, but remember what the noble knights of Camelot have done and who will not be forgotten.

Hail Arthur!"

At that, Rodann lifted his arms to the heavens—and sat down unsteadily—his fetters grating with a piteous sound.

"Your Lordship," said his lawyer—rising to his feet--"the Honorable Crown Prosecutor and I have reached a plea bargain arrangement.

In exchange for dropping the charge of Treason and Conspiracy to Foment Rebellion against Her Majesty, the accused will plead 'guilty' to the charges of kidnap and forcible confinement of persons under the age of majority."

The judge—impressive in his robes and sashes of purple and white—cleared his throat.

"I hereby sentence the accused—Robert Hardy—to serve no less than thirty years of imprisonment to commence immediately.

In light of the psychiatric evaluation by the team of doctors from London, I order that the sentence be served in The Psychiatric Infirmary at Leeds, and that he may not be released until a panel unanimously agrees that he is no longer a threat to Society, and at least 75% of his sentence has elapsed."

The gavel came down like the wrath of God. It was over.

Parents of victims in the gallery wept openly and hugged each other, while outside the courtroom flashbulbs and reporters crowded around the two lawyers--begging for comment.

   ***

"Trevor, I want you to come to Birmingham to see my mother," said Brianna.

"First of all—I want her to meet my future husband. She will be so excited and I think some happy news is just what she needs.
Secondly, I want to ask her about Dad. I just don't think I can do that alone."

"I understand. I just filled the car with gas—should I be saying 'petrol' now that I'm going to be staying and living in England?"

Brianna giggled.
"Call it whatever you want—just kiss me and tell me you love me!"

"I do love you, Brianna. I've waited all these years without really knowing what I was waiting for.
I was waiting for *you*, my darling."

Lady Trethewey was sitting up doing a crossword puzzle when the couple came into her room.
"Mum? It's Brianna."
Brianna was not sure if she was really going senile or whether this was a post-traumatic reaction to her captivity.

She was also not sure what to say about Rodann and the fact that he was in prison and that she was now planning to occupy the family home once more—after nearly 25 years.

"Of course I know who you are, dear. I'm not an old fossil yet!"
"I want to introduce you to my fiancé Trevor Gower, Mum."

"Oh. How do you do?" Estelle said warmly.

Trevor leaned in and gave her a kiss on the cheek—leaving his lips covered with beige powder which Brianna quickly brushed off.

"Gower, you say? There's a Gower in Bristol that Roger used to do business with."

"That was my grandfather," Trevor said.

Brianna nudged him in the ribs.

"Ah, I hope I am not being intrusive, Lady Trethewey, but I want to ask you about your husband, Lord Trethewey," Trevor began.

"He's gone, you know," she said wistfully.

"Well that's what we want to know, Lady Trethewey.
What happened after those brutes abducted you from Broadmoor? Where did they take you?
Basically—what happened to the both of you?"

"It was all so confusing. It was evening and raining cats and dogs and we were hustled into a van and carried off into the darkness.

They put a cloth with something sweet smelling over our mouths—and the next thing I remember is that we woke up in a strange house with strange people.

No explanation or apology was offered, although they gave us a meal and a cup of tea.

We finally demanded to contact our solicitor or the police—they laughed and said that would not be possible.
They said we would be staying here since it was dangerous to return to Broadmoor for some reason.
They said the girls were well looked-after and not to worry.

All very strange!

The next day—or maybe it was two, I don't remember—a well-dressed chap who said he was with the government said that I would be returning to the castle, but that they had to keep Roger 'for his own protection' for the time being.

Again, no word of explanation or what kind of danger we had been exposed to that would require such unusual arrangements.

Frankly, I was more concerned about the girls—due to their tender age and sex.
Roger was ex-military and could handle himself alone.
For some reason, I was not alarmed about the whole crazy situation. I just wanted to go home with my girls."

Brianna sat at the foot of the bed and rubbed her mother's legs and feet.

"So you were separated from your husband and did not see him again?" asked Trevor.

"Well they brought me the news that Roger had come down with pneumonia and passed away.
That was scarcely a month after.
They promised me they would see he gets a Christian burial in the local churchyard.
But I never got any papers from anyone to confirm that was done.
I did get a death certificate by registered post; I've put it away somewhere."

"In the castle, you mean?" said Trevor.

"Yes. Is it important?" said Estelle.

"It will be. We need to see your solicitor about his will and what his wishes were with regard to his estate.
We will need to confirm his death before any of that can be revealed," Trevor said.

Brianna was not receiving the news well.

She sat closer to her Mum and lay her head on her mother's belly and sobbed in gulping breaths like a child would.

Trevor stepped out into the hall and dialed their own lawyer, Mr. Long.

"Can you find out who the solicitor for the family was—or *is*.

I think I can lay my hands on the death certificate but I need to know who composed the will for Lord Trethewey and do they have it?

Yes, thank you, sir."

The nurse came in and said that Estelle needed to be fed and changed, and then perhaps to rest.

The pair kissed her and bade her goodbye.

Trevor held Brianna all the way to the car.

"We need to pay a visit to our castle," said Trevor.

"We need to find that paper."

***

The great iron gate was heavier than Trevor expected as he wheeled the car into the drive by the fountain—which had been disabled for now.

Entering the castle the proper way—through the massive front door—was also new. They had snuck in through side doors and into dim passageways until now.

There was power, however, and Trevor turned on banks of floodlights to illuminate the Great Hall and adjacent halls.

"It's huge!" said Trevor.

"Are you sure there's nobody left here? Nobody's broken in?" said Brianna.

She looked all around her nervously—her senses on alert.

"I don't think so. The front gate was locked, remember? And there are no fresh tire or footprints in the mud at the entrance," Trevor pointed out.

"We've never been on the upper floors—at least, *I* haven't," he said.

"Let's find her chambers and poke around her desk to see if we can find what we are looking for."

Castles aren't like townhouses. The steps are higher and wider and hewn from stone. Climbing a staircase in a castle is like climbing Hadrian's Wall.

Brianna's legs were burning and Trevor was breathing harder than normal.

"Well, we don't need to go to the gym," he quipped. "Just walk around our very own castle."

Brianna kissed him, saying: "I like the way you say *our castle*! Because it *is*, you know!"

Every hall seemed endless in both directions.

"Which way is it?" said Trevor.

"This way, I think," said Brianna.

"Is this hallway lit?" said Trevor, searching for a switch.
He found it and small sconces threw a soft light every few yards down the corridor, making their job much easier.

At length they came to a large chamber— actually a suite of rooms—that had been Lady Trethewey's redoubt for years.

There were sumptuous carpets to cover the floors, large bay windows to allow light in, and a graceful feminine touch to the furnishings in general.

"I can't believe they kept Mum cooped up in here," said Brianna.
"No wonder she walked by moonlight just to get some air."

"Here, Brianna. Take a look at this."

"It needs a key, Trevor."

"Give me a bobby pin from you hair. This might work.

Trevor bent the hairpin open and inserted one end into the lock on the elegant desk drawer.
Anybody who locks a drawer has something to hide he was thinking.

The lock clicked and Trevor tugged the center drawer open. All kinds of papers were strewn inside—nothing seemed organized.

"What we are looking for will have an official stamp or letterhead," he said.

"Like this?"

Brianna had a legal-size envelope with a government stamp that matched the one on the document inside.

Official Record & Certificate of Death
Somerset County Registrar

It named Roger Hardy, birthdate 09-09-1921, born in Shrewsbury UK, as the person whose death had been confirmed by a pathologist—and the cause of death was 'pulmonary failure'.

"*Somerset?*" said Brianna.

"They took my father right out of Shropshire
and held him prisoner far from his home!"

"Fuckers!" said Trevor.
"I can only hope that the men who did this were
part of Rodann's crew.
Because the judge threw the book at them!
Each one got six to ten years in the
penitentiary. Well-deserved, too!"

"He died a lonely death, Trevor, far from his
family and home. It so unfair."

"You're right. Our only consolation is that they
are behind bars, and his wife and children will
again live in peace and happiness on the
traditional Hardy estate.
For that we should be thankful."

He turned to her and took her hands in his.

"I promise you, Brianna, we will restore this
home to its former glory by filling it with love and
laughter and beauty.
That much we can do for your father."

"Yes, darling, you're right. That is what he
would want."

"Let's get this document to the lawyer. I want to
know what your father's will has to say."

                    ***

"Mr. Leslie Swan? I am Brianna Hardy—Roger
Hardy's youngest daughter. Nice to meet you."

They shook hands all around and took a seat in
the solicitor's office—so crowded with books and
papers there was almost no place to put a cup.

"You said on the telephone, Brianna, that you
have the death record—may I see it?" said the
lawyer putting on his bifocals.

"It appears to be in order," he said, removing
his reading glasses and reaching into a drawer to
fetch a fat yellow envelope.

"This is the Last Will & Testament of your
father—Roger Hardy. It has not been amended
nor are there any codicils appended to it."

"Codicils?" said Brianna.

Trevor leaned over to her and whispered:
"Changes."

"I see. Please continue."

"There is a court process required called
probate—in order to put the terms of the will into
legal effect. That includes estate taxes owing to
Her Majesty, of course."

"Of course," said Brianna. "Can we know the general outline of those terms, Mr. Swan?"

"Well, I suppose I can let the cat a little bit out of the bag," Swan said.
"The Beneficiaries include your mother Estelle—naturally—and your older sibling Beryl, and yourself. The estate was to be divided equally amongst you."

Reading, the lawyer went on.

"Title to the family property Broadmoor Castle and its hundred acre allotment goes to *you* Brianna—with a life estate to your mother and your sister."

"He left the castle to *me*?" Brianna was breathless. "*Why*?"

"Perhaps he felt that you would live the longest and being young and sensible, would determine how best to use the property for everyone's benefit.
Without reading too much into it, young lady, I would say your father *trusted you.*"

Brianna was gripping the arms of the chair with whitened knuckles.

"I'm not sure I..." but Trevor took her hand and quietly said: "Let him finish, darling. Let's look at the whole picture."

She shot him a grateful smile and nodded, saying: "Yes, please continue Mr. Swan."

"There is a stipulation that a holiday property in Dorset be shared amongst the beneficiaries, and that title be given to your older sister Beryl."

"Dorset? A seaside property? I never knew," said Brianna.

"At the time of purchase, it was worth £60,000; in today's market I would guess that would fetch ten times that if it were sold," Swan said.

Trevor whistled appreciatively.
"Nice chunk of change," he said.

"Indeed," said the lawyer. "But I'm not done.

There is a trust fund that can now be opened to you in the amount of £25 million.

The good news is that—because it was a trust set up before you reached your age of majority, it is deemed to be a tax-free gift, rather than taxable income.
Put simply, you are now a wealthy woman, Miss Hardy."

Chapter Nineteen   Homecoming

"Your Mother is well enough now to go home," said the head nurse.

"I've had the doctor in charge sign off on it. It's just a matter of coming to get her."

"Thank you so much!" said Brianna hanging up the phone.

"Mummy can come home, Trev. Isn't that wonderful?"

She threw her arms around his neck and stood on her toes as he embraced her, holding as tight as he could without crushing her.

"I've already contacted a firm to clean and restore the inside, and I have a lead on landscapers to renew the gardens and paths," Trevor told her.

I want to build a gazebo and raised patio out back. What do you think?"

Brianna replied: "I think that whatever you want will be just fine with us."

"One more thing. I've spoken to Mr. Long—our
solicitor—and inquired about moving your
father's body to the estate.
    I don't know about you, but I think he would
like to be at home with the rest of us.
    There's a legal process for disinterment and all
the paperwork, but I think we can manage it by
summer."

"I love you, Professor Trevor Gower! I can't
imagine anyone more wonderful than you in my
life.
    And just think! You have found your very own
personal 'Holy Grail'—you have found *me*!!"

Trevor smiled and just looked in her eyes.
    "I can't wait to carry you over the threshold, my
golden dream girl!"

The weather was now full Spring and they
discovered all kinds of surprises—like the rose
garden—now a tangle, but with some care it
would be a showcase for all sorts of roses: English
tea roses, roses from India even.

They found an old orchard with pears
originally from Anjou in France. It was flowering
and would produce fruit, the old gardener
promised.

Amazingly, the exterior walls were sound and
required very little pointing and grouting.

The driveway was resurfaced with gravel and the fountain was drained, sealed and refurbished.

Bill and Beryl found time to come help. Beryl was surprised about the cottage near Bournemouth in Dorset but Bill was really excited.

He always wanted a place by the sea—now they had a getaway for summer weekends when the inn was empty.

"When shall we bring her?" asked Beryl.

"Friday. I think it will all be serviceable by then," said Brianna.

"I've hired cooks and upgraded the kitchen.

They've brought in two enormous new fridges and a separate 40 cubic foot freezer.

The delivery doors that Rodann made use of are just perfect for us, too."

"That's smashing!" said Beryl. "Just brilliant!"

Beryl looked much younger and had a constant smile on her face—even kissed her husband more!

Jeff and Jodie came on Wednesday to see what they could do to help out.

Trevor took Jeff downstairs to the kitchens and cellars, while Jodie went upstairs with the sisters to talk curtains and bedcoverings.

"I want you to help me set up a wine cellar, Jeff.
I don't know nearly as much as you do.
Of course, we'll have a cabinet for Scotch.
I just need some idea where to start.
I've got some dandy carpenters that came highly recommended.
Where do we order the liquor from?
Help me out here, buddy!"

Jeff was in heaven.

"Let's put some cabinets over here..." and the two of them chattered away while outside the evening sun set majestically in the west--limning the turrets and walls of Broadmoor with gold and rose-pink light.

***

Brianna, Jodie and Beryl all walked up the grand staircase that leads to the residential suite on the upper floor.

They were treating Lady Trethewey like royalty—spoiling her with a wonderful reception with flowers and a special lunch.

All she could manage when she saw how her rooms had been renovated was: "Oh, my!"

The carpets were new and the old Persian rugs had been dry-cleaned—which allowed them to keep their hand-woven nap intact while deep cleaning the mold and rot that would destroy them.

Fresh curtains and drapes, newly upholstered furniture—no expense was spared to make it a memorable return for the lady of the manor.

The French doors led out onto the terrace and the carpenters had constructed custom benches and tables which were much more sensible and comfortable.

They did not linger as the wind was cool and the stars out; besides a sumptuous dinner was being laid down in the Great Hall and the smell wafted all the way upstairs.

Brianna gave the first toast in honor of her Mother and thanked her family and handful of guests for their gracious presence.

Trevor rose and proposed a toast to the new lady of Broadmoor—Brianna. He, too, thanked their friends for their unflagging support during this ordeal.

He made reference to Lady Trethewey's moonlight walks on her terrace.

"We saw you floating like a goddess on the water," he said—trying to be poetic.

"Your opalescent gowns and jewellery made
you sublimely ethereal in the moonlight, my
Lady," Trevor said with a little bow to Estelle.

"Oh, I *never* went out after dark, dear. Too
many bugs and bats!"

"I beg your pardon," said Trevor half choking.
"You are saying that you did not walk by the
moon on the high turrets of the terrace?
We saw your figure on several occasions, my
Lady. We found a bracelet belonging to you on the
earth at the foot of a wall!"

"Mummy, tell us it was you!"

"Oh I wish I could, darling girl, but I assure you
it was not me—and I don't sleepwalk!"
Lady Trethewey was enjoying a glass of wine
and Jeffrey was right there to refill her glass.

"Then...who was it we saw? We were not
hallucinating or imagining—we saw a lady in
white as clear as crystal," said Brianna.
"For God's sake Trevor, tell me you took some
photos with your cellphone."

"I'm scrolling...gimme a second. Here! Here's a
couple of shots from our first sighting."

He moved to Estelle's side but everyone at the
table was pushing in to look.

Sure enough! An ethereal form of an older lady with a glittering choker and necklace could be seen against the dark background of night.

Trevor had been clever enough to zoom in on the second and third images.

Everyone gasped; but it was clearly *not* Estelle Hardy lingering on the battlements.

Gratefully accepting another glass of fine French red, Estelle began to speak.

"You know, when I was a young girl, my grandmother spoke about an old tale that concerned my great-great-grandmother—who lived at Broadmoor during the Napoleonic Wars.

It was said that her husband, the fifth Lord Trethewey, was away in France and news came that he had been killed in battle.

The tale said that the night he died he visited his wife in her chambers and made her a promise."

Brianna said: "Don't stop!"

"He promised to come to her on this very terrace, on this very spot every full moon and profess his eternal love.

She died a lonely widow but she believed him-- and every full moon for one or two nights, she would wrap herself in white silk robes, wearing the diamond necklace he had given her when they married, and go to keep the tryst.

It is even said that her last words were: "Take me out for he is coming and I must not be late!"

There was not a dry eye in the house.
And for the rest of the evening the talk was of nothing else.
Especially since the full moon was coming in just a week.
Brianna invited everyone for a White Lady party—at which they hoped sincerely that she would grant them an appearance if they behaved discreetly and quietly.

"Oh my God, Jeffrey! We have to be here!" said Jodie.
Jeff said: "Well, Trevor and I will be loading cases of wine into the new cellar, so I expect that won't be a problem."
He was teasing, of course. He often showed his affection for his wife by teasing her or joking with her.

Everyone said 'Good night' and each stopped in the courtyard archway to look up at the place that The Lady in White was expected to be.

"So there really *is* a ghost in the castle," Trevor said to Brianna after they had gone.

"I had no idea!" she said. "But she is a friendly ghost, I hope, and we will make it clear to her that she is welcome as a member of our family!"
***

"Brianna? It's Jodie. Have you got a moment?"

"Sure I do. What's happening at Abbey Grange?"

"Something's come up and I need your advice.

How about this way? Can you and Trev come round for dinner?
I want both of you to be here on this."

"Sounds serious—are you alright?"

"Yes, yes. It's a decision we need to make and both of you are involved in it anyway."

"You aren't making a word of sense, dear girl, but—sure, we'll come round at six, okay?"

"That was delicious!" said Brianna nibbling on the last bit of Yorkshire pudding.

"I always thought Yorkshire pudding was like rice pudding—a sweet dessert," said Trevor.

"So what did'ya think 'blood pudding' was?" teased Jeff.

"Something gross and disgusting—which it is," he answered.

"Let's get down to brass tacks," said Jeff.

"Something's come up and we're all in a muddle about it," he said.

"Okay. Muddle away," Trevor replied.

"Remember the twins that you rescued from the castle and spirited over here under cover of night?"

"Couldn't forget them," Trevor said. "They were so brave and patient all through that.
I can only hope their parents could know someday how special their daughters really are."

"Well, that's the thing.
Their parents have been killed in a motor accident on the A5 just this week-end past. It was on the news."

"Are you kidding me?" said Brianna. "That can't be—it just can't." Her eyes filled up.

"It's true, love," said Jodie. "The newsman said the twin girls were orphans with no other living relatives to speak of.
Dunno what they're suppos'd to do."

"We could take them in for a bit," said Brianna looking to Trevor for some sign of confirmation.

"I think you are leading up to something here, Jeff—aren't you? What is it you really want to say?" Trevor asked.

"You both know that Jodie and I weren't able to have children of our own. Bad luck, really.
But we talked it over and we wanted to ask the lawyer if it were possible to adopt them—both of them."

Jodie added: "We really got on well with the pair of them here; you remember how distraught I got when we had to let them go."

"Yes, we do," said Brianna. "You do forgive us for that don't you? I mean they couldn't stay, could they? They were missing children with a family out looking for them."

"I know. I know that," Jodie said.
"This is a bit of a strange situation: a couple with no children who badly want to care for these girls who have no parents.
Like a plot twist in a bloody novel, isn't it?"

"So if I'm hearing you right—you want to apply for adoption and you want me to ask my solicitor

if that is legally possible—one, and *two*, practical
and reasonable," Trevor said.

"Well—*you* tell us if it's practical and
reasonable—or just daft, the last resort for an
aging couple who want to tuck children into bed at
night and have them know they are loved," said
Jodie.

"Has anybody thought about what the kids will
say? Or want?" said Brianna.

"That's a sticky point," said Jeff. "I mean how
does one go about asking such a thing to children
still in shock and mourning their parents?"

Jeff poured himself a Scotch and passed Trevor
a beer.

"How?" Jeff said again.

"I don't think it's going to be as hard as you
imagine it will," said Trevor.

They already know you, and trust you, and if
you lay it out for them so they know that you want
to be their family now..."

"Trevor's right," Brianna said.
"You have a safe and comfortable home—with
horses no less! If the court will approve it—I
really think it could work out very well!"

Brianna was getting enthused by the whole scenario.

"And we'll be the auntie and uncle, won't we Trev?" she said.

"I don't have a problem with that," he replied.

"I'm so glad you're optimistic with this," said Jodie. "This is one of the biggest decisions we've ever had to make.

But we've made it, and Jeffrey and I are both committed to being the best parents we can be."

Brianna hugged Jodie, murmuring words of encouragement.

Trevor and Jeff started on a second round and both wore a not-so-hidden smile that said that the men were very much okay with this.

"I have spoken with the Crown Ward who has temporary custody of the children," the lawyer Long said to them the next day in his office.

"I can proceed right away with the application and—subject to approval, the custody will transfer to the Earl and his wife and it will be entered in the record that they are the legal guardians and parents of the said infants."

"'Infants' meaning children under eighteen," said Trevor.

"Precisely. Now I think it prudent and appropriate that a conference be held with the girls themselves, just to confirm this proposal is what they want, too," said Long.

"Can you set that up," said Brianna.
"I'll ring you later when I have an appointment with the caseworker. Is this still your phone number?"

Brianna and Trevor were hopping with excitement.
"Oh, Trev! Isn't this just perfect? What are the odds? I feel dreadful for the girls to be suddenly without their own parents.
Bit honestly—I am thrilled that they will get to be with Jodie and Jeff! It's the rainbow after the storm!"

***

"Hello Emma, hello Christine! Do you remember us? Jodie and Jeff?"
Jodie was smiling with a hint of pink in her cheeks.

"Yes, of course. You were so nice to us," said Emma.
"And your horses are gonzo!" said Christine.

"Let us start out by saying how very sorry we are about your parents.

No one deserves to lose their family in that
way," said Jodie.

"We just got away from that wretched castle!"
said Emma—starting to cry forlornly.

"I know. Just getting back to normal.
Do your teachers and friends at school know?"
asked Jodie.

"We haven't said anything, but I s'pose they've
seen the news on the telly," said Christine.

"Well, Jeffrey and I wanted to talk to you."

Jodie suddenly felt awkward like it was a first
date or something.

"We very much enjoyed the time we had you at
our house—at Abbey Grange.
We missed you terribly after you'd gone.

So Jeffrey and I wanted to know if you would
like to come live with us—as...well...your family.
We would be a family."

Jodie paused. Jeff took over.

"I think it would be smashing to have you come
and stay with us. We could have such fun!
I've got a dozen plans for things we could do—
build a special family room for pingpong or piano

lessons or just watching the telly on the biggest
screen ever!”

Jeff was so animated! He was getting up--then
sitting down--and squirming all around.

“You could help me with the horses,” he
continued. “They’re a bit of work, you know.
Can’t just ride ‘em and leave them on their own.

They need brushing and washing down, and
somebody to speak their names gently and feed
them apples and carrots.
I really can’t do it all,” he said in a half serious
voice.

Christine ran to him and threw herself in his
arms and said breathlessly: “I can help you, Jeff. I
even remember their names!”
Jeff removed his glasses and wiped his eyes.
“Do you now? Do you indeed?”

Emma came over and sat beside Jeff on the
couch. But her head was turned to Jodie.

“We won’t be any trouble, I promise!” said
Emma.

That was more than Jodie could bear and she
rushed over and lifted Emma on her lap—even
though she was eight and not at all tiny—and

started to straighten Emma's hair and kiss her along her hairline.

Then Brianna started to cry and soon everyone was swept away by the emotions—even Trevor turned away to blow his nose noisily.

The caseworker signed a document that she was satisfied that the applicants were suitable candidates for the adoption of Emma and Christine Thompson.
An official copy would be sent to Mr. Long and the adoption would take effect at midnight Sunday March 11th.

The twins moved in on Saturday.

They each got their own room and they each were invited to make suggestions for redecorating and personalizing their rooms—including the washroom shared by the two rooms.

Christine was jumping on the bed. Emma was admiring the view from her bedroom window.
The whole broad landscape of trees and meadows and the little pond could be seen and she lifted the casement window to let the air of a new day in.

"This is *my* room," said Christine proudly.

For years the girls had shared--but things would be different from now on.

Each girl pretended to be the Lady of the House in their respective spaces, and demanded that everyone—including Jodie and Jeff and Brianna and Trevor--ask permission before entering their private territory.

On Sunday midnight, the girls were sound asleep but Jodie and Jeff were on the couch—Jodie laying contentedly in Jeff's arms, her eyes sparkling with utter delight and joy.

"Thank you, Jeffrey," she murmured.

"I am so pleased for us, for this blessing," he said in return.

At length, he rose and lifted her bodily from the couch and carried her to bed.

A great peace lay on Abbey Grange that night.

***

So it was at Broadmoor Castle—the dark energies dissipating with the winter ice that was dripping from cornices and turrets in long icicles.

The pond was clearing and ducks were noisily mating and seeking nesting sites.

The gardeners were doing double duty: pruning and clearing years of rubbish and bramble from paths and gardens.

Then putting in bedding plants—some perennials like hostas and ivy, and some flowering annuals like marigolds and salvia.
Red geraniums would follow with silvery 'dusty millers' that traced the curves of the garden.

Both Estelle and Brianna approved of Trevor's plan to construct two greenhouses on the property for growing flowers and some vegetable from seed.
The hothouses had louvers and vents to allow the plants to harden off—once the danger of frost was past and they had attained a healthy two to three inch height.

All of this had commenced at once and there was a coming and going of vehicles at the south gate bringing supplies and soil, sawdust and sand.

"Trevor," said Brianna at breakfast. "There's someone's been forgotten in all the fuss," she said.

Trevor wracked his brains but came up empty. "Who is it, darling?

"Amanda Brixton. The girl who was Rodann's toy and Mother's handmaid. She told us she was tricked into coming here and then restrained in leaving. She was as much a prisoner as anyone!"

"Right! I remember! What's happened to her?" Trevor said.

The police turned her over to the County social worker since she is penniless and homeless.
Unlike the other children, she has no parents, no home to return to.
I suppose they've put her up somewhere until she finds a job—or moves on.

"And you are thinking we could have her here to look after Lady Trethewey—since she is familiar to her and obviously dedicated to ensuring she is well taken care of," said Trevor.

"What do you think?"

"I think we could manage it, see how it goes," Trevor replied.

"Can you give the solicitor a ring while I talk to Mummy to see how she feels about it?"

"On it, boss!" said Trevor affectionately.

Brianna took his collar on both sides with her slender hands.
"Will you promise to always be so cooperative with my demands? she said.

"I don't see why not!" said Trevor.
"Marriage is teamwork."

"Then kiss me and promise me, then take me out of this place for a few hours—I'm getting bored sitting day after day with nothing to do."

Trevor swept her up in his arms and did as he was requested.

Just then a tradesman or perhaps a farmhand knocked and they opened the front door to an extraordinary sight!
"Where'd ya be wanting these animals, then, Miss?"
Three young men were standing over wire cages—two with chickens and one larger one with a pink pig.

Brianna looked at Trevor.
"Did you order these?"

"Not I," he replied.

"Where the hell are we going to put them?" said Brianna.

At that moment Lady Trethewey descended the stair case and said in a cheerful voice:

"Out beside the greenhouse, dear. I've
instructed the carpenters to build a pen for the pig
and a chicken house adjacent to it.

We've got to have fresh eggs, and eventually
home-smoked bacon. It makes such a difference
to country living, don't you agree?"

Brianna and Trevor were laughing, and walked
the men around the north wing and into the area
where the carpenters had been building.

Once the animals were comfortably bedded in,
one of the farmlads gave them the rundown on
their basic needs and how to collect eggs, and how
to keep the henhouse in order, etc. etc.

After they were gone, Brianna and Trevor
walked to the car.
Brianna gave Trevor a playful look and said:
"*You* get to muck out the pens and cages; *I*
collect and rinse the eggs."

"You mean just because I'm a man—I get to do
the dirty work?" he said.
"Just because you're *my* man," she answered.
She flicked her tongue over his lips and
scampered to the car.

The new king of the castle—a bantam
rooster—let a lusty 'cock-a-doodle-dooo' loose
that made them wonder: 'What next?'

***

"You'll have to fill out the paperwork," said the County clerk in Social Services. "And there's a fee."

"A fee?" said Brianna with a tone of surprise.
"We're giving one of your charges a job and a home, so you should be grateful that we are taking a burden off the back of Shrewsbury Social Services," Brianna said indignantly.

"Sorry, Miss. Rules is rules."

They brought Amanda in and she greeted them warmly.
The dour old social worker in charge of her case said to Amanda:
"Don't be any trouble. The good Lord must've taken a liking to ye to give ye a chance like this."

"Thank you, Mrs. Barnes," said Brianna, taking Amanda by the arm and swiftly leading her out to the car park.
Trevor was waiting and started chatting with Amanda right off the bat like they were old chums.
Once safely home, Lady Trethewey was delighted to see her and went immediately upstairs to help Amanda settle in and get organized.

"Who says there's no such thing as 'happy endings'? said Trevor.

"Well there is *one* more thing on our to-do list, my darling," said Brianna.

"We have to turn my common-law spouse into a lawfully wedded husband!"

Chapter Twenty   Springtime of the Heart

"We've got to see the lawyer, Brianna" Trevor said.

He's got the property deed all ready for you, and once it is signed—you are finally the legal owner of the estate."

"Oh, it will be over at last!" she said. "Can we stop by Abbey Grange on the way home. I need to see Jodie."

"No problem. Let's grab a bite in town first. I am starving!"

"Are you saying I don't feed you enough, Professor Gower?"

"It's this country air, my love! My appetite is double what it used to be."

"That's because you're in *love*, silly man!"

The appointment was over in ten minutes.
It was done.
Broadmoor was secure in the hands of its rightful owners.

"Let's pick up some Shrewsbury cakes to take
to the Grange—I know a lovely bakery that makes
them according to the traditional recipe. It's not
everyone that knows how to do that these days,"
Brianna said.

"Lovely to see you two," said Jodie. "Oh!
Shrewsbury cakes! Haven't had one in ages!

Jeffrey? Come have a Shrewsbury cake!"

"We have a wedding to plan!" said Brianna.

Let's get Beryl and I would like Amanda to be a
part of it, too," she said.

"Oh? You've got that girl back? She was very
nice to your mother I understand," said Jodie.

"She still *is*," said Brianna.

"Now. Let's begin with the service—then work
backward," she said.

"You act like you've done this before," teased
Jeff.

"In a woman's mind, Jeffrey, she goes over her
big day again and again—so that when it finally
arrives, she is calm and ready!" said Brianna
calmly.

"So do the men have anything to say about
this?" retorted Jeff.

"Yes," said Brianna. "The men can discuss how
they're going to pay for all this!"

Jodie guffawed and Brianna tilted her nose up.

"Cripes! I need a drink," said Jeffrey, looking for any excuse to sample the great scotch Trevor had brought home last month.

The ladies wandered off into the back patio and were furiously scribbling notes and sipping white wine spritzers.

Nobody seemed to notice the age difference between the couples—they were family, and that was *that!*

***

The next week was a flurry of activity—buying a dress and shoes and matching handbag, arranging the flowers and a photographer, a caterer for the reception at Broadmoor.

Trevor and Brianna had settled on St. Giles Church in Abbey Foregate, Shrewsbury.

The church was historic and charming—the Rector Father Brown—was too; he must have been eighty if he was a day, but his congregation loved his sermons and he did marriages as well.

"It's a good job he's Anglican as well," commented Jodie—referring to Trevor. "Could've been a Catholic!"

"The same thing, really," replied Brianna.

"Your father would not have approved it if he were!" said Jodie.
"D'you think Jeffrey would have married me if I were from a different denomination? Fat chance! His mother would've died a lot sooner if he had done!"

Jodie was in an excellent mood. So many bright new things to celebrate!
The children—first and foremost. They were a constant source of delight and merriment for both Jodie and Jeffrey.

And now—the wedding of her niece and her lovely man from Canada!

"What am I going to wear?" asked Trevor after dinner.
"Have you no clothes? No, of course not. You came from Canada with nothing but an old scroll and a few socks in your suitcase," chided Jodie.

"We'll get you a tux at the men's shop in town," she said.

"Speaking of...does yours still fit you, Jeffrey?" she continued.

She couldn't stop talking. She really couldn't.

"Do you think the invitations will reach everybody in time?" asked Brianna.

"I'm sure they will," assured Jodie.

The bigger question is whether Father Brown will now be expecting to see us for Communion every Sunday," she said.

"Jeffrey and I have been awful about attending church."

"Don't worry, my pet," responded Jeff.

"We shall put in an appearance from time to time. I want the girls to go to Sunday School.

I will send Father Brown a nice fat cheque for the Renovation Fund and he will appreciate that!"

"I can't believe it!" said Brianna. "In five days I shall be married!"

Jeffrey was to be the 'best man'. Beryl deferred to Jodie to be Maid of Honour. She and Bill were so shy they just wanted to warm the pew.

Emma and Christine were bridesmaids, of course.

They endlessly rehearsed their roles up in their rooms and could be heard chiding each other for any little perceived slipup in their performances.

It would be a small wedding at the church.
It was the reception that was going to be the event of the season.
Even *The Chronicle* and *The Star* would send representatives.

But the three ladies—accompanied by Lady Trethewey—had matters well in hand.

The biggest bother was the food and drink of course.
Amanda was an extra pairs of hands at the castle since she knew her way around, knew every cupboard and closet, and was thrilled to be included as if she were family and could be heard singing way down in the scullery.

"Plan for fifty," became "Plan for a hundred."

The groundsmen worked double shifts to get the lawns in shape and put up a great tent in the back for the guests to serve themselves.

Finally, the Big Day arrived.
A limo picked them up at Abbey Grange and delivered them to St. Giles at eleven on the dot.

The aisle had bouquets taped to each of the pews, the organist was playing Bach *Air On A G-String*, but when the couple arrived she switched to Mendelssohn's *Wedding March.*

Brianna looked radiant, her golden hair pinned up and off her slender shoulders.
Her dress and train were like swan feathers fluttering around her lovely figure.

If people gasped at this goddess of Beauty it was covered by the notes of the pipe organ.

At length, all was still and Father Brown began to speak the words that every girl longs to hear in her life.
His voice was remarkably vibrant for such an elderly fellow, and it seemed but a moment until he recited the words:
"Do you—Brianna Hardy—take this man to be your lawfully wedded husband, to have and to hold…?"
She had to steady her voice.
"I *do!*" she said.
"And do *you*—Trevor Gower—take this woman…"
Father Brown stepped back and said:
"Here in the presence of God and the assembled witnesses, I now declare you husband and wife."

Brianna didn't wait for Father Brown to even finish the next sentence!

She threw herself into Trevor's embrace and kissed him, and kissed him again.

Beryl said later that for a moment she was afraid she wouldn't stop kissing him.

And they were but thirty seconds married!

The weather was fine with bright sunshine and a light breeze from the north, and the photographers muttered about 'how good the light was' and 'good job it wasn't raining like the week-end before', and so on.

The limo came and took the bridal party straight to the highway that led into the hills—and Broadmoor.

***

Amanda greeted the party at the front door and it was clear that the Great Hall had been set up with tables and chairs and loveseats—a bartender had set up an indoor bar and soft music was playing.

Outside the tent was erected and food servers were laying tablecloths and cutlery out.

Special mood lighting and more speakers for the music had been cunningly placed so they were not obtrusive.

The party barely had time to change before guests started arriving.

There was a special valet present tonight to park the cars—allowing guests to simply enter.

It was Terran!

At the request of both Lady Trethewey and
Jeffrey, Earl of Trent, the judge gave Terran a
suspended sentence for his courageous efforts in
helping Brianna and Trevor escape with the twins.

He—along with his mates in the small company
hired to set up and manage the event—were
nicely dressed and glad to be a part of everything.

Brianna was now wearing a black cocktail
dress which set off her blonde locks perfectly.
Her mother gave her a necklace that was a
family heirloom that complemented the dress.

"Diamonds are a girl's best friend," said Estelle
as she fastened the clasp around Brianna's neck.
The hall was dimly lighted but the gemstones
sparkled as Brianna was preparing to go down.

"Wait!" said a male voice from the shadows.

Trevor stepped out and took her in his arms.

"I asked you a question long ago that you
promised to answer one day," he said softly.

Brianna's eyes widened.

"You promised to tell me how *Wildswallows* got its name," he continued.

"Oh," she said. "'Wildswallows' was the name we girls came up with as a symbol of freedom and happiness that we hoped would come to us someday.
We went through such a dark time. The symbolic meaning behind the name gave us something to hold onto, to hope for."

She looked up as the warm amber glow from the lamp caught the angle of his jaw, erasing the shadow under his eyes.
She spoke almost in a whisper.
"Today is that day," she said.

Trevor nodded ever so slightly.

"I want to get pregnant, Trevor.
I want a child with you—a child that will give both of us hope and certainty that Love will give the 'wild swallows' a home at last!"

And with that—they turned, and glided down the staircase into the sweet presence of true love.

The End